What Lies Beyond the Hollow Grove

S.E. Van Meter

This book is dedicated to Ruby Jones's Blood Bucket bar. Thank
you for intriguing me and scaring the hell out of me.

Editor: Brian Paone
Cover art & interior graphics: Kyle Lechner
Formatter: Kari Holloway

IISBNs
Paperback: 978-1-7344523-2-7
eBook: 978-1-7344523-3-4

Chapter 1
New Frontier

The Wiley G. Estates finished construction in 1957. The project developers boasted it would be the new frontier of family living. Fifty-two years later, Wiley G. Estates remained in the southeast corner of Bradford … but the promise had died. The families who had once thrived had either moved or had passed away. The residents who inhabited the neighborhood now were considered by most to be less than ideal people. Seamus Van Leer was constantly reminded of this as he stood on the porch of his own depreciated house.

Seamus looked left toward the Hermann's cluttered property that sat before the dead end. The overgrown grass covered numerous plastic gas cans and rusted lawn equipment. Seamus often wondered how John and Pat's feral children didn't injure themselves while traversing the lawn.

Seamus shuttered while turning right toward the Buckland property. It was equally overgrown. Seamus scanned the shared driveway where his silver Toyota Camry and Greg Buckland's purple Plymouth minivan sat.

"You call this the New Frontier?" Seamus scoffed.

His mood shifted to darker territory once his gaze fell on his morning coffee. He wished he could spike it. After further consideration, he realized that would be a terrible idea. Alcohol was not only his coping mechanism but also the cause of his sorrow.

Seamus was twenty-one and still living at home when the accident had happened. Seamus and his parents were drinking buddies and didn't share a parent/child relationship. One Friday afternoon, after working with his father, Randy, they had driven to Trixie's Drive-Thru for some beer to celebrate Seamus's completion of his ninety-day probationary period.

The Van Leers had drunk fast upon returning home. Through lack of better judgment, Seamus had started for the front door to get more beer, but Randy had told him to stay home; Seamus was still wet behind the ears and couldn't hold his alcohol as well as he and Ida could, or so Randy had thought. Randy and Ida had gone for the beer instead. Just as they had stepped from their home on Grover Street, Seamus had fallen asleep on the couch.

The sound of thunderous pounding on the front door had awoken Seamus. He had shot up like a rocket. The stale taste of beer had violated his mouth as he stood and struggled for composure. On the opposite side of the door had been Deputy Paone, a well-known face to the Van Leers. Whenever one of them violated a traffic law, Deputy Paone was there to cite them.

"What's going on?" Seamus had asked bitterly.

"Your parents were involved in a collision. Your mother veered left of center on Donaldson Road and collided with the Elnors. There were no survivors." Deputy Paone had masked his true feelings. *If only your parents would have learned from their past drinking and driving incidents.*

Seamus had fallen to his knees after hearing the news.

That had been the beginning of the dark times. Seamus could not afford to live in his family home any longer, so he had sold it and purchased his current home, where he has lived miserably for the last nine years. Residing amongst the *garbage of Bradford* was what he owed. Despite his self-inflicted punishment, Seamus couldn't help but to feel disgust. He possessed two virtues his neighbors lacked. He was hard working and felt guilt for his actions.

Most of the residents who lived in the subdivision bilked the welfare and metro housing systems. The place was a dumping ground for trash, figuratively and literally. But the worst residents were the pill heads. Once in possession of their pills, they crushed and snorted them. Seamus had overheard his neighbors refer to this as doing a *bean*. Seamus didn't understand how they arrived at the term, but that was the slang they used, as drug deals were commonly made in the streets.

Seamus could not dwell on his parents or neighbors. It was Friday, and he had an appointment with a job placement worker at the Bowling County Job and Family Services. In a single gulp, he drank his coffee and felt the raw burn.

He strolled through his shoebox living room into his kitchen to place his mug in the sink. Feeling that time was getting away, he grabbed his resume hanging from a refrigerator magnet and dashed to his bathroom to change. The coffee boosted him as he walked toward his car. *The sooner I can get this done, the sooner I can enjoy Memorial Day weekend*, Seamus thought before a voice broke his concentration.

"Hi, Seamus."

Seamus looked left and saw Lynette Buckland sitting on her porch glider, while her mongrel dog lay motionless. "Hello, Lynette." Seamus mustered a polite response.

Lynette tucked her weak, zit-covered chin toward the top of her white halter top with *Party Girl Princess* adorned on its front in pink letters. She acted cartoonish and bashful when Seamus made eye contact. She raised her left knee to her body, resting her bare foot on the glider.

Seamus gained an ample view of her crotch through her yellow cotton short shorts; she wasn't wearing any panties. *Goddamn, what a pretty pussy,* Seamus thought, mesmerized.

Guilt gripped him as the thought passed. Seamus had known Lynette since kindergarten. During their youth, she had struggled socially and academically. She was an overtly thin and shabbily dressed girl. Her rabbit-like face and bucked teeth further accentuated her homeliness. When Lynette and Seamus were in elementary school, he had always thought of her as an annoying nuisance. She had been in every class with him, and the teachers had always grouped them together.

A few days before starting the fourth grade, Seamus had ridden his bicycle to Graham Elementary to check the classroom roster taped on the main entrance door. He had been pleased to see Lynette would not be in the same class. She had still been listed on the third-grade roster.

Lynette repeated the third grade for a second time before finally passing. It wasn't until high school when they had crossed paths again. Seamus had been in his junior year, and she had been a freshman. At the beginning of the school year, Lynette's mother, Kathy, had died from complications of weight loss surgery. Shortly after her death, Greg had started doing odd jobs for the old widow, Ellen Sergeant. Greg had exploited Ellen's kindness and had convinced her to leave her house to him upon passing. By the time Greg and Lynette had moved into the house, Lynette's body and libido had exploded with maturity, and she had built an extensive reputation from the local boys as *one hell of a practice girl*. Seamus remembered the local boys saying that about her as he stared from across the driveway.

Lynette stood from the creaking glider and approached the edge of the porch, staring at him with deep infatuation. "Watcha' doing, Seamus?"

"I have an appointment. I should be heading out."

Lynette eyed her bare feet and tucked her chin toward her chest while raising her right heel off the porch, acting cartoonish and bashful.

Seamus watched as her cotton shorts rode up, and her hips swayed. Despite her unattractive face, her body was perfect. *If I wasn't dating Elizabeth and I could get past her face, I'd take her back to my house.*

The screen door behind Lynette flung open. Lynette stiffened as Greg stepped out. Her flirtatious expression melted away.

Greg glared at Seamus. He gritted his few remaining brown teeth as he advanced. Greg appeared more dingy than usual. His salt and peppered hair and beard was covered in filth, and his tan-colored shirt sporting the words *This is Not a Gut, It's a Shed for My Power Tool* was tightly exposing the bottom half of his gut. His belly hung over his ripped, paint-spackled jean shorts. He clamped an angry hand on Lynette's shoulder. "Get your ass inside!"

Lynette scurried away, embarrassed and defeated.

"We ain't gonna have a repeat of last time. If some horny sonofabitch comes sniffin' around here and wants your goods, he's putting some *goddamn* money on the table!" Greg bellowed.

Seamus knew who Greg was referring to. A few months before the plant closure, a coworker eleven years older than Seamus and Lynette, Todd Lawson—who everyone referred to as Mr. Barely Legal—talked Greg into allowing him to take out Lynette. Although, anyone who knew Todd's reputation knew what his version of a date would entail.

Seamus's and Todd's lockers were next to each other, and, on numerous occasions, Seamus had seen stacks of *Hustler Barely Legal* magazines inside.

Seamus loathed Todd; he viewed him as an aged biker douchebag. Todd sported a salt and pepper mullet and a Sam Elliot mustache. Todd's sense of style solidified Seamus's opinion. At the age of forty-one, Todd was in full predator mode with a particular taste for the vulnerable. Lynette was perfect prey.

A week leading up to their date, Todd had told his friends he would take Lynette for a hamburger at the Rawling Springs McDonald's and conclude the date with a visit to Jeff Carr's scrap lot on the outskirts of town. Todd had added the seclusion made for a prime hotspot. Todd had bragged about past conquest, boasting he and his rusted Dodge Ram—which he referred to as *Old Green*—had seen more young beaver than any horny teenager.

At the beginning of the following week, Todd had divulged the details with three of his buddies in the locker room. "So, I told her stupid old man I had taken sweetness to Lynette, and the dumb bastard let me scoop her up like nothing. I had to keep my word that I was taking her out on a date, so we went to McDonald's. I stuffed a burger down her neck. After that, I had the pedal to the floor all the way to Carr's lot."

"I bet the burger wasn't the only thing you stuffed down her neck," one of Todd's grungy companions had added.

"Can I finish telling the fucking story? I was just about to get to the good parts," Todd had barked. "I had a hard dick all the way there. I couldn't wait to get inside that idiot … willing or not. As soon as we got there, I had her panties down and rammed her good. I'm glad I got that vasectomy; that pussy felt *soooo* good raw-doggin' it. Hell! It felt even better when I cream-pied her. The only regret I have was I didn't get to fuck her in the ass. It was still fun looking at the fear on her ugly mug as I gave it to her."

After listening to Todd's horrific story, Seamus had slammed his locker door and stormed out. Seamus remembered what Lynette had endured after the so-called date. Seamus had been watching television and drinking beer that evening when he had heard the aftermath. Seamus's paper-thin walls allowed him to hear everything outside.

Lynette had sobbed as she climbed her porch steps. The sound of Todd's truck speeding away had followed. The next thing Seamus had heard was the Bucklands' screen door striking the house. Greg had screamed with fire in his voice. Lynette had pleaded with her father not to hurt her. The sound of a leather belt connecting with flesh had followed. Lynette had taken abuse twice that evening.

Seamus and Greg exchanged glares as he opened his car door. The sight of Greg became intolerable. With a firm hand, Seamus reached for his gear shift and placed his car into Reverse.

Once backed onto Observation Drive, Seamus could still feel Greg's hateful eyes. Seamus did not afford the grungy bastard any more attention as he passed Neptune Drive. While he drove, his vision was further polluted from the condition of the houses in the neighborhood. The houses on Saturn Drive were nearly falling down; most had blue tarps in place of windows. The houses on Mars Drive had sustained heavy fire damage, likely caused by botched drug manufacturing. Most of the houses on Venus Drive were in the midst of being demolished. Seamus felt like he was leaving a war-torn dystopia.

Seamus turned right onto Church Street. While heading east, he surveyed the surrounding neighborhood. The houses were not much better than the ones in his neighborhood, but compared to the houses located in the Wiley G. Estates, they were stately manors.

He turned left onto Railroad Street and headed north. The intersection of Grover Street was just ahead. Each time he stopped at the intersection, his heart sank. Sadly, he remembered a different time when his parents were still alive. Not wanting to revisit the past, he accelerated with haste. Seamus needed to be focused.

Seamus drove promptly to the next intersection at Main Street. He turned left without regarding the stop sign. The village limit was just ahead, and Rising Sun Rubber sat to the right. Even though the factory had only recently closed, it looked like it had been abandoned for decades. While working there, he had never regarded it as anything more than a job, but now, it resembled something from a nightmare. Main Street became Paulding Pike as he cleared the village of Bradford.

The rural area surrounded him as he looked toward Hoyle before making a right onto Donaldson Road. "Fucking snobby Hoyle pricks, I bet those rich fucks never had to experience a layoff," Seamus grumbled. His heart beat like thunder as he approached State Route 14.

The traffic was heavy with commuters. A feeling of gratitude washed over him, despite the inconvenience of busy traffic. His attention was dedicated to something else, not on the section of road that lay ahead. The last thing he wanted was to imagine his parents' vehicle and the Elnors' sitting mangled.

Just as the traffic gapped, he gunned the pedal and sped west on State Route 14.

Nervous sweat rested on his brow. His breathing became shallow as he headed toward Rawling Springs. Realizing he must look distraught, he lowered his sun visor and checked his reflection. *Jesus Christ, I look like a goddamn train wreck.* Seamus frantically groomed himself, only affording partial attention to the road. This was a foolish thing to do, but Seamus wasn't known for common sense.

Surprisingly, Seamus arrived safely at the intersection of State Route 14 and Krotz Road. While turning right onto Krotz, he felt his appearance was satisfactory. *Good enough for whom it's for.* Seamus had to pay special attention; this area was usually populated with deputies. The last thing he needed was to get pulled over. Knowing his luck, it would be Deputy Paone. Seamus drove responsibly as the Bowling County district buildings came into view. Seamus winced as he recalled his youthful visits. Jenson Drive abruptly appeared after he passed the juvenile detention center. The Bowling County Job and Family Service parking lot sat behind the old county courthouse. It was good to be heading there instead of the other places that had sculpted his youth.

Seamus found a spot in the back of the lot and parked. Confident posture was what he tried to convey as he stepped from his car, but it was a ruse; fear of rejection plagued him.

A hazy film of depression hung in the waiting room. Some patrons were shrouded with the burden of finding work, while the others were waiting to see their welfare caseworkers. Avoiding eye contact as much as possible, Seamus sauntered to the third row of plastic seats. As he blindly sat and looked forward, his eyes were met with the large green eyes of an overweight boy.

The boy had disheveled dirty-blond hair—both in color and condition—and he sported a faded *Captain Power and The Soldiers of the Future* t-shirt, neon-orange shorts, and torn-up Nike sneakers that looked two sizes too big. Sticky brown patches covered the boy's hands and mouth. The patches were likely from a fudge-pop that he wore more than consumed. "My name is David. I'm ten, and I can't read," the boy said, lacking modesty.

"I'm charmed to make your acquaintance, David," Seamus muttered.

"My mom and her boyfriend are here for the lady who gives me my stupid-person check."

Seamus contorted his face.

David raised his pudgy hand and reached for Seamus's resume. "What's that paper?"

Seamus pulled away his resume.

Just as Seamus was about to scold David, a bellowing shout came from the right side of the room. "Get over here!" David's mother screamed and scowled at him from across the room.

Seamus thought she resembled the piglike women who live on Saturn Drive.

The obese woman sported a tightly pulled ponytail that strangled her unwashed hair, a stained white Garfield the Cat t-shirt, purple sweatpants, and yellow Crocs shoes. Three additional children circled her like vultures as she sat on her mobility scooter. When David reached her, she yanked him over her barrel-shaped leg and delivered machinegun spankings. "How many times do I have to tell you? Stop telling people our business!"

"I bet that kid's father wished he would've gotten a blow job the day that kid was conceived," Seamus said, hoping to gain a laugh from the person sitting next to him. Seamus was only met with silence.

Sitting next to him was a dirty, frail old man rocking back and forth. He wore a filthy overcoat, brown work pants, and black Velcro tennis shoes with no socks. He mumbled through his rusty beard, "Pop that you can't stop!" as he rocked. He paused to look at Seamus before starting again. "Ski-bop-a-dop!"

Seamus grew uncomfortable. Nervously, he panned to see if others were looking. Surprisingly, no one was paying attention. Seamus wished he could escape the situation. Luck smiled as he heard a female call his name from the front of the lobby.

Seamus observed the old man before making his way. "Good luck, old-timer. Out of all these worthless bags of shit, you seem to be the only one who actually deserves the government dough. Hell, even if you're faking, that kind of acting deserves something."

The old man uncrossed his legs and emptied his bladder.

Seamus watched as the wet spot widened. "Nice touch, old-timer."

He walked to the front of the room and approached a glass partition that separated the employees from the people sitting in the lobby. As he looked through the smudged glass, he saw an old woman sitting behind her desk studying him with prejudice eyes.

"Seamus Van Leer?" she asked in a cracked voice.

"Yes, I'm Seamus." He gagged on her overbearing scent that permeated through the holes in the glass.

"Holly will meet you at the door to your right. I'll buzz you through."

Seamus acknowledged her. *I think Grandma Moth Balls and Grandpa Piss Pants need to go out for a night on the town.* The door buzzed and swung open.

Standing in front of Seamus was a short, full-figured, wavy blond-haired woman wearing a pant suit. "Hello, I'm Holly McPherson. I'm your employment agent." She spoke in a bubbly tone, proffering her hand.

Seamus returned the gesture.

Holly led him through the office cubicles to her workstation.

Seamus couldn't help but to ogle her posterior. *It's a bit on the thick side, but I'd still bend her over and give her the business.*

Holly turned and gave him a pleasant yet nervous smile as they arrived at her desk.

Seamus took a seat. *Privileged fucking cunt wouldn't know how to handle this dick. She's probably married to some nine-to-five asshole.*

Holly's desk donned a Rolodex calendar with patronizing positive quotes, a schedule planner, and a couple framed pictures—one displaying two Aryan blonde children. One was a girl around ten, and the other was a boy around seven. The second picture was of Holly and her husband. Seamus scoffed while Holly looked perplexed.

"Sorry. I must've had a tickle in my throat."

Holly looked onto her computer. "I appreciate your determination meeting with me today despite not feeling well."

They sat in silence as she opened numerous files on her dual monitors. The silence gnawed on Seamus's nerves as her expression grew cold.

She turned her attention from the screens and wrote notes on a 5"x 8" notepad. Holly looked at Seamus, displeased. "I see that ten years ago you registered with the department. Have you made any other employment efforts since that time? Have you acquired your high school equivalency?"

I knew this would bite me in the ass. Maybe if I give it to her straight, I can gain some sympathy. "I knew this would come up," Seamus said, defeated, as Holly leaned closer. "I did register here ten years ago. It was around the time I was expelled from high school during my senior year."

Holly's gaze grew prejudicial.

"I had some troubles growing up in Bradford. It's not your typical small-town hamlet. It's a knock-down, drag-out place."

"I don't understand what you're getting at."

"I was always bigger than the other kids, so naturally, they wanted to make a name for themselves. Not to brag, but most kids win some and lose some. I never lost."

"Mr. Van Leer, I hardly see how neighborhood scraps hold any bearing to you not receiving your high school equivalency."

Seamus shot her an angry glare before relaxing his face. "My apologies, but I didn't finish. As I said, while growing up in Bradford, I never lost a fight; however, these fights led me to numerous visits to juvenile court. During my senior year, the judge advised that it would be in my best interest to attend vocational school at Penguard and learn a trade. He thought it might occupy my mind and put me on the straight and narrow path. It was the kindest thing he ever did. Things were going good for a while, at least until I met Chris Rayle Junior. After the second semester started, I was attending autobody shop when I watched Rayle and his buddies pounce on this smaller kid. When that happened, I just saw red. I threw Rayle's buddies to the side, but when I got my hands on him, I lost control of my temper. After the teacher pulled me off, I realized I must have pulverized Rayle's jaw. It was the closest I'd come to losing a fight. Junior must have gotten a lucky shot on me just above

my right eyebrow, leaving me with this little forget-me-not."
Seamus pointed to his eyebrow.

Holly indulged Seamus to see where he was going with all of this, if anywhere at all. Her thoughts drifted on how she would handle this buffoon while she maintained her attentive guise. *This must be the dumbest person I've ever dealt with in all my time as a job placement worker. Even if he had a high school equivalency, I couldn't see any respectable employer taking him on.*

"Anyway, after I was expelled, I got a job at the Amoco in Bradford until it eventually closed. After that, my dad got me a job at Rising Sun Rubber. Between working there and doing overtime, I didn't have time to get my GED. I just thought the place would stay open long enough for me to retire. I figured I didn't need my diploma."

Holly regarded Seamus with abhorrence. "That was unwise."

"Is there anything you can do for me?" Seamus asked submissively.

"I doubt it. I can't refer you to trade benefits or truck driving school because of your lack of diploma. Besides, the only place hiring is Moline Medical Warehousing, but those positions require a high school equivalency. However, there's a third-party company that does business there. It's a janitorial company. JanStar. What were you making at Rising Sun Rubber?"

"I was making fifteen on the hour."

"The starting wage at JanStar is only eleven dollars, and they don't offer benefits. Would this be something you'd be interested in? If you choose to do so, I highly recommend you return here and enroll in the Capable Program to earn your GED."

Seamus nodded a single time.

"I think it's your best option. I'll get you an application." Holly stepped from behind her desk and toward another associate's cubicle.

I may not have a diploma, but if I had you, I would have that pussy quivering. Seamus watched as she sashayed away.

Holly returned and handed Seamus a shoddy-looking application. It was not centered, nor was it detailed.

Hell, I think a fast-food application would look more professional.

Holly handed him a pen, and he filled it out.

"Here you go. It's all done." He slid the pen, application, and resume toward her.

"Good. It could take a couple weeks before they get back to you. I know it's not what you were earning at your previous job, but it's the best we can do for now." Holly stood and extended a weak handshake.

As Holly bid him a good day, Seamus sized her up. Seamus did not conceal his glances as she cringed. He relished her repulsion as he stepped into the waiting room.

The frail, old man was still sitting there.

Seamus smiled and pointed at him while cocking his thumb in a finger-gun manner.

The old man smiled at Seamus before rambling on again. "Shabbily dap the fat TAAAAAAPPPP!"

"Mr. Clancy! Would you please settle down? Your caseworker will see you soon," the old woman barked from behind the glass.

"Mr. Van Leer! We would appreciate it if during future visits you don't encourage Mr. Clancy!"

"Settle down, bone bag. By the time I come back here, Old Hobo Joe will have joined the choir eternal. By the looks of it, you'll probably be with him."

The old woman sat with her mouth agape as Seamus stepped out.

Clouds covered the sky, casting grey dread, as the wind pummeled Seamus's face and swept through his black hair. He leaned forward while traversing the wind. Frantically, he clicked his key fob as he aimed it toward his car.

The forceful winds had devastated him. After catching his breath, he lowered his sun visor to check his reflection. Seamus's crowning glory was his only feature he indulged modest vanity toward. He retrieved his hairbrush from the armrest compartment and groomed his hair; he stared with hardened concentration on his reflection.

Seamus loathed his face and critiqued it as his gaze lowered. He started by judging his chin; he always regarded it as overtly pointed. His ridged jawline was also unpleasant to his eyes. Seamus felt the same about his eerily placed cheekbones and boney forehead. Seamus ran his finger along the scar Rayle had given him. This was the face of a man with a rough life.

His expression softened when he spied his thick hair. Elizabeth Krantz found his hair attractive, which made him appreciate it more. Seamus rested his head against the headrest and silently reminisced the night they first met.

CHAPTER 2
BLOODY GRAVEL ON A MISTY NIGHT

On the Friday night eight weeks prior to his layoff, Seamus made a trip to the Hollow Grove Bar. On that evening, Seamus met Elizabeth and found love. However, earlier in the day, Seamus's mood soured due to the mass meeting before the end of his shift. Prior to the meeting, rumors spread like wildfire on what it would entail. The rumors were confirmed as the employees assembled. The facility was, in fact, closing. Upon arriving home, he heard his rowdy neighbors bickering. With tact, he pushed the sounds from his head.

Dreadful thoughts consumed him as he sat in his recliner. Aside from his house, his job was his entire world. As the hours passed, he found he could not stand his own company. Seamus marched to his bedroom and changed from his work uniform into a plain white t-shirt and black jeans. He slid on his black metal-tipped boots along with his leather jacket.

Seamus studied his reflection in the mounted mirror on the closet door. While not regarding himself as a handsome man, he did enjoy his wardrobe selection. Standing at 6'3" with a solid build, his reflection reminded him of Packard Walsh, his favorite character from *The Wraith*. An arrogant smirk rested on his face as he retrieved his Marlboro Reds and bull-skull Zippo from the nightstand. Seamus only indulged in smoking when he drank; he intended to do both.

The sound of his neighbors bickering greeted him as he stepped outside. The Hermanns were arguing over who took the last of the pills and who smoked the last of the grass, while Greg screamed at Lynette for being a whore. Previous experience dictated that when both families argued amongst themselves, they would spill out and feud with the other neighbors. It would be a good resolution to tie on a few drinks so he could sleep through their feuding.

Once in his car, Seamus backed away and shredded through Wiley G. Estates. He drove with narrow determination, wanting only to get away. He only stopped briefly at the intersection of Railroad and Main. Railroad Street became Bradford Road when he passed into the flat, rural area.

When the opportunity arose, he hammered the pedal while crossing State Route 14. A few country houses rested on both sides before he entered the wooded area. The tall trees on both sides extended their branches over top of the road, giving the feeling of traveling through a tunnel. The steep downgrade on Bradford Road lay ahead. Seamus jetted the pedal to speed through it. The stop sign at the intersection of Bradford Road and Hollow Ridge Road rested shortly after. Hollow Grove Bar sat across the road to his right.

Loose stones flew as he cut across the intersection toward the parking lot. Seamus eagerly steered to the north side. He stepped out and approached the brown solid board fence located to his left. Seamus paused to peer through the section of fence with the missing boards. Strange items sat before him on the property. Two shimmering tubes, seven feet wide, rested on their sides, supporting an unusual object. The object looked like a strange, quasi-futuristic apparatus. It reminded him of the rubber autoclaves at work. However, the device only appeared similar in shape. Seamus could not swear to it, but he thought the object possessed rocket thrusters. It was hard to determine, as overgrown grass concealed its bottom. *Jesus, I haven't had a drink yet, and I'm already seeing shit.*

After he passed the fence, the cobblestone wall of the bar lay ahead to his left. The streetlamp in the right corner of parking lot nauseated him as the artificial light shined. After his eyes adjusted, he looked up toward the white vinyl-sided second floor. In the center was a diamond-shaped window. Strange lights emitted from it. White, green, purple, and blue flashed. He lowered his gaze and looked forward. After he rounded the corner left, the entrance came into view.

Upon entering the bar, Stevie Ray Vaughan's "Crossfire" pounded through his ears. It was a fitting song for a roadhouse bar. At first glance, the place did not appear to be packed. The stage, dance floor, and most of the tables and chairs were vacant. A few regular patrons hung around the jukebox, along with some of the rougher clientele throwing darts. The rowdy patrons threw darts around each other, while their companions prayed the darts would not strike them. The bartender, Bob "Mack" McManaway, shouted at them to knock it off. One of the patrons playing darts was someone Seamus was unfortunately familiar with: Carlton Sweeney.

Seamus focused on the centralized bar counter.

Carlton, commonly known as Sweeney, hammered darts at the wall as each of his lackeys took turns standing. Sweeney looked the same as he did when he and Seamus had first met. He sported a red flattop and wore the same dirty white pocket t-shirt and camouflage pants, along with steel-toed boots. Seamus did not want to draw attention, but he glanced at Sweeney's shirt. The blood stains were still present from their previous confrontation when Seamus had pummeled him a few weeks back. Sweeney didn't notice Seamus; his attention was dedicated on two women standing by the pool tables.

One woman was a well-dressed blonde in her mid-twenties, and the other, who also appeared in her mid-twenties, was a raven-haired woman wearing a black leather jacket with a white low-cut blouse. She also wore tight midnight-blue-colored jeans that hugged her shapely hips. Her black leather boots reached the bottoms of her knees. Every time she bent over the pool table, she made great strides to emphasize the gesture. Sweeney paused to watch her with undivided attention.

Fucking pathetic asshole. Seamus sat on the red barstool and acknowledged Bob with a brusque greeting. Most patrons never called Bob McManaway by his first name; they called him Mack instead.

Mack stood behind the bar and blew an exaggerated sigh through his horseshoe-shaped mustache. He grabbed a rag from under the bar and wiped the sweat from his bald head.

"Hey, Mack, how are things?" Seamus asked.

"Good until you showed up," Bob said, half serious and half joking.

"The atmosphere is always so cheery. I swear it should be a members' only establishment."

"That's not a bad idea. If I do that, I could keep out riffraff like you and that jacktard Sweeney, especially after the shit you two pulled."

"The way I remember it, that sonofabitch was the one getting belligerent. If anything, I'd say I did you a service."

"You could've killed him, from what I heard about your little parking lot scuffle. I'm surprised you didn't shatter his fucking jaw. Did you have a roll of quarters in your fist?"

"I just popped him with what God gave me."

"I don't need a goddamn murder in or around my establishment. Speaking of which, hold on a damn minute. Hey, Sweeny! Knock off that dart bullshit or you'll be carried out horizontally!"

Seamus looked back toward Sweeney and his friends.

Sweeney chuckled but complied. He grew bored with darts, and his attention was now occupied with the women.

"What's your poison, Seamus?"

"I'll take a double shot of Jack and a bottle Busch Light."

Seamus drank slowly. He regarded Sweeney's presence and felt it would only be a matter of time before Sweeney realized his. After he slammed his double shot of Jack Daniel's and gulped his beer, he felt an elbow brush his left shoulder. Seamus looked up and saw Sweeney leaning over the counter. Seamus cut his eyes at him.

"Hey, Mack, I need a pitcher of your cheapest shit. There's some prime wildlife just begging to be fed."

"Keep your shirt on, asshole. I have other customers. Don't pull any of your typical horseshit. One more fuckup and I'll ban your ass. Do you understand me?"

"Loud and clear, Mack. I'm just trying to get some stink on my cock. I think the blonde is little Miss Prissy, but that black-haired one looks like she could go off like a rocket, and I want to be the launchpad." Sweeney chuckled before he looked down at Seamus. "Sup, Shea? I didn't see you there."

"My name's not Shea, Sween."

Mack traded glances at both men. "I'll only say this once! If any of you clowns exchange blows, I'll ban both of you!"

"I'm good, Mack," Seamus grumbled.

"I'm just here to wet my whistle, Mack—both of my whistles if I'm lucky, as long as tough guy stays out of my way." Sweeney strode away to resume his conquest.

Seamus turned to watch.

Mack looked with disapproval and set down another double shot and a bottle of Busch Light. "You mind what I said. If you cause any shit, I'll split your skull."

"I'm cool, Mack," Seamus grumbled. He raised his shot glass and consumed it without a single flinch. Seamus knew there would be action.

Sweeney returned twice, each time requesting another pitcher and nudging Seamus harder.

Seamus understood Sweeney intended to have business.

"Hey, Mack, I need another pitcher and quarters for the jukebox."

"What's got your knickers in a twist?"

"That sexy little number is going to do a pool table dance!"

"If she rips the felt on the table, I'm taking it out of both of your asses! I run a respectable joint, not a goddamn sleazy strip club!"

"Come on, Mack. We're just having a good time, and besides, I think a little pussy on display might brighten up this dump."

Mack slammed down the quarters.

The coins rested only a second before Sweeney gathered them.

"Have your fun, but if that bitch starts taking off clothes, I'll call the law!"

"Don't worry, old-timer. I don't want to share the bitch with anyone. That cunt belongs to me. Hell, maybe if her prude friend loosens up, both will be parked in my bed."

"You mind what I said, Sweeney!" Mack shouted as Sweeney raced toward the women.

Sweeney's friends sat next to the dartboards with their attention solely on the women.

Sweeney excitedly added quarters to the jukebox.

Much to his own resentment, Seamus's curiosity bested him.

The blonde was infuriated, while the raven-haired woman appeared drunk.

Seamus placed his bottle on the bar counter, strode toward Sweeney and his crew, and folded his arms.

"This is a bad idea. I won't be a part of it," the blonde protested.

"Come on, Laura. This is why everyone thinks you're frigid. Let's give these guys a show. Come on girl. *Whoooo!*"

"Find your own ride home!"

"Go ahead and leave. I'll get her home safe!" Sweeney hollered.

Laura glared before storming out.

One of Sweeney's friends shouted, "Cock-teasing cunt!"

The raven-haired woman climbed onto the pool table.

Sweeney chuckled as he stood by the jukebox before making a hurried selection, then sat on an empty stool as the jukebox played Buckcherry's "Crazy Bitch."

Seamus watched as the men leaned in their seats, looking like small children captivated by a birthday party clown. *Pathetic.*

The raven-haired woman moved with experience. The only thing missing was a stripper pole.

Seamus shifted his attention from the men to her sexually charged dance.

She pulled off her leather jacket and tossed it gingerly to Sweeney. She raised her eyes from Sweeney and looked at Seamus.

She was struck with unwanted clarity. Two overwhelming thoughts passed. The first was a strange sense of attraction. It was not the same type of attraction she felt toward numerous men (and women alike). After it passed, the second most distressing thought came—a feeling of interlocking destiny. What did it mean? She gathered her senses and returned to her party girl state, moving with determination.

The men whooped and hollered, becoming rowdy with instigation. The song ended, and they requested an encore while demanding her to remove more clothes.

She fell motionless while they persisted.

Mack burst from behind the bar. Before he approached the girl, he snatched her leather jacket from Sweeney with a loud *thwop*. Mack shot up his arm and ushered her down.

She eyed Mack with fear and gratitude, then shifted her gaze toward Sweeney's group.

Sweeney stared with a disconcerting fixation. When the soles of her boots landed on the tiled floor, Mack shoved her jacket toward her with brutish force.

The need to escape enveloped her. She hoped Mack would assist.

Mack did not honor her silent request. *You brought this upon yourself. You made your bed, and it looks like you'll be lying in it tonight—with Sweeney.*

Her eyes glossed with desperation. She swallowed hard and stepped backward, hoping the men did not see her nervousness.

The men exchanged whispers.

Hoping not to draw attention, she reached into her pocket for her phone. Luckily, she found it. She needed to leave … now!

Mack glared at her. "It's high time you get out of here."

She turned and made for the front door.

Mack passed Sweeney's group as they huddled together.

"Looks like your bitch baled," one of the grubby men said.

"Yeah, dude, it looks like the only thing you're getting your sticky-icky on is a magazine," the other grubby man added.

The third smaller man kept his mouth shut.

Sweeney's hubris culminated as he flew from his chair, and it to skidded across the floor.

The smaller man sunk low. "Ah shit, Sweeney, we were only kidding."

"Yeah, bro, we were only just jerking your chain," the second added.

Sweeney was too far in the scope of his ego to listen. "You fucks think I can't have her? I'll show you how a real man gets what he wants. You chicken-shit bastards will be the ones tossing off later. Not me! Just think, when I was done with her, I was going to let you guys have a shake. Fuck that! It looks like she's all mine!" Sweeney turned away from his friends.

"Did you stupid fucks really have to egg him on? You know how he is. I'm not going to crash and burn with him or with you stupid motherfuckers. I'm bouncing out," the smaller man said before trotting out.

"We've got to get out of here. I don't want to go down with Sweeney."

"You ain't shitting. Let's get the hell out of here!"

The men left with worried haste.

Seamus bit his lip with frustration. *Looks like I'll have to play hero.*

Mack shook his head.

Upon stepping outside, Seamus noticed a car speeding away north on Bradford Road. The darkness and heavy mist prevented him from identifying the occupants. Seamus saw the raven-haired woman standing under the streetlight and next to a red and white Ford Lariat F-150, talking on her phone.

Sweeney stood with his back against it, shouting. Of all places she could be, she was standing by Sweeney's truck.

"Chelsea, you and Josh need to get me now! This crazy stalker won't leave me alone."

"Stalker? Bitch, I ain't no fucking stalker!" Sweeney thrusted his torso from his truck and tried to grab her wrist but missed with his clumsy effort.

She and Sweeney locked hateful eyes as she slid the phone into her pocket.

Sweeney snorted like a bull before making another attempt. He wrapped his arms around her and spun her around as she pounded on his chest. He thrusted her against his truck's grill, pressing his meaty hands against her breasts while working his slobbering mouth on her neck.

She refused to scream, screaming would only excite him.

Sweeney delivered pelvic thrusts as he spread her legs with his knees.

Seamus sped with fury in his steps toward Sweeney and the woman. Once he was behind Sweeney, he clawed his left hand, honing it like a talon, for Sweeney's thick neck.

Sweeney reared backward while maintaining his hold on her. He screamed with pain and rage while Seamus pulled him away.

To Seamus, it felt like pulling a parasitic organism from a host. The thought disgusted him.

After the uncoupling, she dodged right and hung to the ground.

Seamus spun Sweeney around and pressed his back against the grill of his own truck.

Sweeney was met with three cracking blast and followed with a crushing blow to his nose. He rained blood on the damp gravel, cupping his face.

Seamus turned Sweeney around and jabbed him with a crushing kidney punch.

Sweeney arched his back, screaming with a thunderous roar.

This allowed Seamus the opportunity to bring the pain a final time. He slammed Sweeney's face into the hood of his truck twice. The first strike followed with a thud. The second was accompanied with a crack. He placed his leg behind Sweeney's legs and threw him to the ground.

Sweeney landed facing the sky. Droplets of blood flew to the side of his head, landing on the gravel. He tried to shimmy to his feet but fell back.

The raven-haired woman's mouth was agape with amazement. Seamus remained silent as she panned his figure. Men had fought over her before but never like this. Was this the sense of destiny she felt? Who knows? But one thing was sure, she was his tonight. The violent display of force awoke something inside her. The raw power made her tingle.

Seamus looked at her but not in the same manner. His anger cooled as the red hue dissipated from his sight. "Are you all right? Did he hurt you? I didn't hurt you, did I?"

"Not at all," she said, taking her wits back.

"Good. Maybe you should go back into the bar, or at least stand by the front door until your friends arrive. I don't think he'll be a problem, but you should still go. I should get out of here too." Seamus turned and walked away. By the time he reached the cobblestone wall, he slowed his pace. Once next to the brown fence, he heard a voice.

"Hey wait!"

Seamus stopped. The call was followed by the clopping sounds of boots. *Clop, clop, clop, clop.* He turned to see the raven-haired woman running. Watching her was exquisite, as her breast bounced under her shirt.

She arrived panting. "I never got your name.

"I don't recall giving it."

"I'm Elizabeth. Elizabeth Krantz."

He remained silent as he sized up her voluptuous body before resting his gaze on her crescent moon-shaped eyes.

"Look. This isn't the movies where you can play hero and walk away. This is real life; a woman wants to know the name of her hero."

"My name is Seamus. Seamus Van Leer," he responded in an accidental James Bond-esque tone.

She inched closer. "That's an interesting name."

"It's an Irish name. My mother was full-bloodied Irish, and my father was full-bloodied Dutch." He looked over her shoulder as Sweeney stirred and did not afford her attention as she advanced. His attention was on Sweeney alone. He looked back at Elizabeth's wanting eyes and made a quick decision. He remained cool without making her aware of Sweeney.

Elizabeth shifted her gaze to the top of his head. "You have beautiful hair. I've never seen such a beautiful crop." She extended her fingers toward him, looking fascinated, and grazed her fingers through his scalp.

"Instead of talking about the origin of name or my hair, why don't we get hell out of here? Besides, it would save your friends the trouble of coming to get you. Where do you live?"

"I live north on Bradford Road. It's a little village called Milbridge. It's about ten or fifteen minutes from here."

Seamus watched Sweeney in the distance tuck his knees into his chest and curl into a ball. He didn't know what Sweeney's motives would be if he stood. Would he stumble into the bar, enter his truck, or take notice of Elizabeth and want to fight again? If that happened, Seamus feared the fight would turn deadly. He smiled reassuringly at Elizabeth as he moved his hand toward the middle of her back. He opened his passenger door for her and shuffled her inside. As Seamus entered his car, he noticed Sweeney start to stand. He rammed the gearshift into Drive and turned northbound onto Bradford Road.

Elizabeth and Seamus sat quietly as they traveled. She reached for her phone and called her friend to let her know that she no longer needed the ride. After ending the call, they cleared the remaining wooded section of Bradford Road.

Seamus panned the area through the mysterious evening mist, then spied the Eisenhower Cemetery, which had an ominous yet appealing appearance. The illusion of the mist made it look like a floating island surrounded by trees and a wrought iron fence. The damp retaining wall glistened in the night. After he cleared the cemetery, the road drastically went into a downgrade before they crossed an old sky-blue truss bridge.

Elizabeth could no longer stand the silence. "Are you enjoying the view?"

"Yes. I didn't realize how nice this area is."

Elizabeth rolled her eyes, as she couldn't gain his attention. She decided to acquire it through different means. She peeled back her leather jacket to expose her cleavage, then raised her leg and rested her foot above the glove compartment. "State Route Forty is just up here, and it's a pretty busy road, so you'll have plenty of time to look at the scenery … inside and out."

Seamus's gaze fell on her as they waited to cross.

She exposed more of herself and made inviting gestures with her mouth. Her sexually playful nature captivated Seamus. "I think it's clear. We're not far from my house."

Seamus accelerated with haste.

"Whoa, big fella. We'll get there soon enough."

"Sorry. I guess I was a little distracted."

"I think you were more than just a little distracted."

Eventually, they arrived at the intersection of Bradford Road and State Route 345, and the Milbridge village limits came into view. They passed the sleepy dark houses before approaching a railroad crossing with three rows of tracks.

She told him her house was to the right just after the tracks.

Seamus was eager to turn, but she scolded him as he saw a dirt road to the right that ran beside the tracks.

"Don't turn yet! Turn right after the trees!"

Seamus surveyed the dirt road; it was an endless void. He heeded her instructions and turned right into a low-dipping cul-de-sac lined with cinder blocks on both sides. After curving left, he faced Bradford Road. A khaki-colored split-level house rested to his right.

They stepped out, and Elizabeth walked up a small set of concrete steps leading to a door that rested between the house and a breezeway.

Seamus told her he wanted to smoke a cigarette before entering. In truth, he wanted to learn the layout.

She told him it would be fine if he smoked inside.

Seamus declined and watched her enter. Keeping to his intentions, he reached for his pack of cigarettes and Zippo. He lit it and approached the garage. Behind the garage sat a large pond. He noticed the cattails sticking above the water as it met the land. Taking a deep drag, he turned from the pond and walked past his car. A light caught his attention from the window to the left of the side entrance door. Seamus watched as Elizabeth removed her jacket and placed it behind a chair.

He passed the window until the cul-de-sac straightened. A cluster of trees sat in the interior island to his left. He stopped when he arrived at the main road, and his attention was drawn to a mailbox that displayed the numbers 28808 on the side. It was an easy number to remember; 288 was the prefix of his old phone number at his parents' home. His cigarette burned down to the filter, and he flicked it out in the road. He climbed the side entrance steps and pulled the door open with zeal.

The darkness of the garage enveloped him. Once his eyes adjusted, he turned left and climbed the steps leading into her kitchen.

Elizabeth sat at the kitchen table with her back to him.

Seamus stepped softly behind her and looked over her shoulders and down her shirt.

She turned and smiled playfully. "Why don't we head upstairs? I think you and I have a matter of personal business."

Seamus offered her help to stand, but she declined.

Elizabeth extended her hand back and led him through a wood-finished dining room, then into an elongated living room where a curved staircase sat in the center. She tugged on his hand firmly as she sashayed up the stairs. She deliberately moved a few steps ahead so he could see her tight rear.

They entered a hallway at the top of the stairs. To the immediate right was Elizabeth's bedroom. She stepped through the doorway, turned on the light, and strutted to an oak wardrobe. "I have something I want to show you."

Seamus sat at the foot of her bed and looked out the window. His mind gravitated to the large pond.

"Hey! I have something to show you! I think it'll be more interesting than the view out my window."

"I bet it's a great view to wake up to every morning."

"Uh yeah, it's pretty impressive, but I see it every day. If you like good views, let me indulge you." She opened the wardrobe doors and stepped to the side.

Seamus was taken aback. Resting on the interior hooks of the right door were one-piece, high-cut, dominatrix costumes with matching leather hats. Hanging on the hooks of the left door were an assortment of weapons, such as cat-o-nine tails, paddles, and a variety of riding crops.

She contemplated the riding crops and pulled one down. She held it with her right hand like a saber while tapping the business end on her left. "This is my favorite."

Seamus had seen some of these items before at XXX-Ray's Adult Books and Novelties, but to see them in someone's house was a different experience. There was an array of other bondage devices resting on the lower shelf. Some of the items looked aggressively used, while others looked custom made. The items he could not identify were the ones that disturbed him the most.

She returned the riding crop to its hook and grabbed a ball gag from her treasure trove. She walked toward him, determined.

Seamus leaned back and stood. "I'm not a goddamn sissy boy."

Elizabeth had fire in her eyes. She stood on the balls of her feet, ready to pounce. She dashed in front of the doorway as he was about to leave. "Where the hell do you think you're going?"

"I don't play that submissive shit."

Elizabeth concealed her fervor as she sized his body. She grabbed his collar and placed a hand on his crotch. "You have a nice piece of pipe." She pushed him backward while maintaining her grasp on his collar. Her strength was incredible. She ripped off his shirt.

Before he realized it, his boots were off, followed hastily by his jeans and underwear. Seamus wanted to remove her clothes, but she refused.

"No! You don't get to take my clothes off!" She backed away and removed everything. Her pale skin, pert breast, and curvy thighs made him want her more. She sensed his urges and rebuked. "Sit the fuck down! I don't care if you saved me! This is my house and my rules!"

"What the fuck is wrong with you?"

"I want you to put on your boots before I ride your cock. If I can't dominate you, I at least want you wearing something leather." She placed her hands on his chest and pushed his back down. She straddled and received him as she bounced.

Seamus reached to cup her breast but was denied.

She grabbed his wrists and pinned him down. "Don't even think about coming. I'm going to use you as I see fit," she whispered before biting his earlobe. She cried out as she lifted herself and looked into his eyes. "I'm going to come. I want you to come with me. I want to feel it!"

The moment Seamus released, she arrived with a shouting climax. Her vocal display made Seamus release harder. With each pulsing throb, she reacted. She sat on top of him, catching her breath. She brushed her lips on his with a teasing kiss. She positioned herself on her left side with her back to him while she faced the window.

Seamus inched toward her.

"If you want to cuddle, turn off the light first."

Seamus gently stood and switched off the light. He returned and fell asleep shortly after.

Sometime later in the evening, or perhaps in the early morning, a flash of bright lightning, followed by a crack of thunder, awoke Seamus.

Elizabeth remained asleep as the lightning continued.

Seamus loved watching the storm while cuddled to her. It was bliss. A part of him wanted to wake her so they could watch it together, but he didn't know how she would react. He stayed awake long enough to watch the storm.

The following morning, he awoke, and Elizabeth was gone. Feeling achy, he sat upright, and swung his feet over the bed. His lower back shot with a flash of pain. Bending to retrieve his clothes was agonizing. Seamus realized he was still wearing his boots. Feeling a little foolish, he corrected the situation and dressed. It had been a considerable amount of time since he'd last had sex. This probably attributed to his body aches.

Descending the staircase was a taxing labor, but when he heard Elizabeth's voice, he perked up.

"Yeah, it got crazy last night. The stupid-looking oaf really scared me, but that Shea guy pulled me out," Elizabeth said casually.

Seamus didn't hear another voice, so he assumed she was talking on the phone.

"I expressed some gratitude for saving me and giving me a ride home. I better go. I'm sure he'll be waking up soon. I'll see you and Josh later. Bye."

Seamus approached her. "Seamus. That's how you pronounce my name."

Elizabeth flashed a smile and ushered him to sit. She wore a short, white, low-cut cotton robe with the word *Pink* stitched on the rear. The word appeared again in smaller text above her right breast. Elizabeth was fully nude under the robe.

She rolled her eyes as he looked. *Hasn't this dumb ox ever seen a naked woman before?* She closed the front of her robe.

Seamus rattled his head. *I can't believe I had her last night.*

Elizabeth scoffed and turned her back to him before reaching for a pack of Marlboro Reds and the bull-skull Zippo that sat on the kitchen table next to her phone.

"You smoke the same cigarettes I do. I also have a lighter just like that."

Elizabeth regarded him with an *are you that daft?* expression. "It should look like your cigarettes and lighter, because it is your cigarettes and lighter. I couldn't find mine, so I checked to see if you had any."

Seamus felt a burst of anger but suppressed it. He didn't want to blow the deal. He was putty in her hands. He reached across for his cigarettes and lighter.

Elizabeth turned away as Seamus did his best to express a confident conceit. She smoked the rest of her cigarette at nauseating speed. She stood silently and felt as he caressed her.

Seamus thrust his member between her buttocks. Before long, he was engorged.

I hope he doesn't get worked up. Last night was one thing, but I don't know if I want to make this a regular thing. She bent over to extinguish her cigarette in the ashtray as Seamus increased speed. She flattened her palms on the table.

This feels so fucking good. I thought I was lucky last night, but to have it twice in a row. His hands grew restless and descended under her robe knot as they navigated between her legs.

Elizabeth reached for her phone and stood. Playtime was over. Elizabeth opened her phone and eyed him with an uncomfortable smile. "Where did the time go? It's ten to eleven.

I have to get around. My sister Greta is coming over to pick me up. We have some running to do."

"Where are you heading? If you don't want to inconvenience her, I'd be happy to help!"

Elizabeth searched for a response. "It's okay. Her husband has my car and is doing some engine work. Greta and I have girl-time when he works on it. It's nice to have an honest mechanic. He went to Penguard when he was in high school."

Seamus looked solemn.

Elizabeth didn't know what she had said to achieve this but did not question her luck.

"I understand about wanting some quality time with your sister. Family is important. Would it be alright if I get your phone number?"

Elizabeth shifted from her left to her right, pondering. "Why don't you give me your number? I'll put it in my phone and text you later."

This was not the response Seamus had hoped for. As he told her his number, he leaned in with tact. Relief swept over as she put his number into her contact list. When she rose, he resumed normal position.

"I've really got to get around. I'll message you later when I have time." She ushered him toward the door.

When his nose almost touched the door, he turned around. "Would it be alright if I had a kiss?"

She hurriedly nodded and gave him a partially opened-mouth kiss. She watched as he closed his eyes dreamily. After she retracted, he kept his eyes shut in ecstasy. Elizabeth stifled a chuckle before turning her concentration to his hair. "Okay, lover boy, it's time to go. I'll message you later, okay?"

Seamus turned and stepped through the door. He felt light as a feather as he stepped down the first step. By the time he stepped down the second, he heard a tapping on the door window behind.

Elizabeth stood with her robe pulled back. She blew a kiss and followed with a playful wave before pulling the blind.

Seamus walked esteemed. As he sat behind the wheel, he blew her a kiss before pulling away.

Upon entering the Wiley G. Estates, his mood hardened as he crept along Observation Drive. He parked his car and stepped out. Once he was on his porch, his phone chimed. It was a text from Elizabeth. *Hey hero, I wanted to say thanks again. Maybe I'll hit you up sometime* ☺

CHAPTER 3
STONE COLD

Two cold thoughts occupied Seamus's mind. First, he considered the few and far between visits with Elizabeth. They had always begun with her requesting a ride. The second notion pertained to sex. It always happened after he had fulfilled her traveling needs and never before. Seamus wondered if it was motivated by affection or out of obligation.

Seamus sought for a diversion and looked to the horizon. Without checking the time, he figured Elizabeth should be awake. She worked late and slept in. During their time together, he had never asked her where she worked. That question would have to wait. Right now, he needed to talk to her. Seamus pulled out his phone and selected her number. After the fourth ring, he heard her voice. "Hello."

Elizabeth sat at her usual place at the kitchen table. Her opened robe exposed her frontal nudity as she smoked her first cigarette of the day. The smoke masked the cotton-candy-scented body spray that permeated from her chest. It was a loathsome fragrance. Her manager, Pauly, requested all his entertainers wear it. Pauly boasted that the clientele enjoyed it. One gentleman in particular raved over it.

"Baby, you smell sooo damn good," the gray-haired man had stridently said over the sound of his loud exhaust as he and Elizabeth had sat in his minivan.

"Thanks. The boss likes it and so do the other gentlemen," she had said, wondering just how desperate she was for a bean.

"I'll give you a five milligram, like we had agreed, for the private lap dance earlier, but I'd gladly give you another one if you'd come home with me. Come on, it's not that far away. I live in Bradford. There's plenty of bean to go around there. I have a solid hook up." The creep had revealed his stained teeth.

Elizabeth had scrambled for a response as she checked the time. *Where the hell are Chelsea and Josh? "The owner has strict rules against his dancers providing private parties. Ten years ago, one of his clean-up girls went missing after she had agreed to do a private party. Pauly said if he caught any of his girls doing that, they wouldn't be allowed back. You don't want me to lose my job, do you? I think you'd miss me."*

"You're right, sugar. I'd miss you." Greg had handed her the pill while leaning closer and extending his arm behind her headrest.

"I'd miss you too," she had said, gagging.

To her luck Chelsea and Josh had arrived in his red Pontiac Sunfire. *Saved by the fucking bell.* Elizabeth had flung open the door and slithered out. She had strode toward Josh's car while stuffing her phone in her pocket and retrieving her cigarettes.

Once she had lit a cigarette, she had placed the pill inside the cellophane. Elizabeth had ridden in silence.

Not wishing to focus on last night's events, she lit another cigarette and tried to shake the thought. When she was halfway through smoking, she stood and walked toward the kitchen cupboard. She grabbed a clear glass plate and set it on the counter, then reached farther into the cupboard for a razorblade. She set it on the center of the plate and carried the items to the kitchen table.

Elizabeth crushed her cigarette and brought the bean from the cellophane. She placed it next to the razorblade and grabbed her purse. She sifted through her wallet and found a twenty-dollar bill. Elizabeth's eyes gleamed while she pressed the edge of the blade along the center of the pill. Just as it split, the sound of her phone jostled her. The phone chimed as she quartered the pill and crushed it. *Fuck! Of all times!* She placed the call on speaker. *Paradise is right in front of me, but I have to entertain this asshole … Fuck!*

"Hey, baby. How are you?" Seamus asked.

Elizabeth rolled her eyes. "I'm okay."

"I just finished my appointment. It went okay. I might have a job."

"Well, there you go." She forced a perky response.

"It isn't the greatest job. It's at a warehouse, but I won't be working for the company; it's for a custodial company instead. Regardless, I need the job."

"Well, it's always important to get the things you need," she said as she made six lines.

"I really need your company."

"I can't. Josh and Chelsea are coming over, and I already have plans," she said, knowing her statement would crush Seamus.

The few times Seamus had been exposed to Chelsea and Josh, he had expressed strong jealousy. Seamus snidely referred to Josh as Long Blonde Josh. Elizabeth paid close attention as she listened for quiet curses. Seamus would be crawling with rage if he knew Long Blonde Josh and Trashy Chelsea—whom Seamus believed to be bisexual—would be there. Elizabeth didn't hold any true feelings for Seamus, but for some reason, his jealousy made her glow. Unfortunately, he did not exhibit any.

"It's okay if you have plans. I hope you'll get a hold of me soon."

"Okay. Talk to you later," she replied briskly before flinging her phone across the table. Elizabeth stood, untied her robe knot, and grabbed the plate.

Josh and Chelsea should be awake. Even if they weren't, she had the perfect persuasion.

Josh and Chelsea sat with their chests exposed and their backs against the headboard.

Elizabeth looked at Chelsea first when she entered her bedroom. Chelsea's red-highlighted hair was disheveled, but she still was still an image to behold. Elizabeth studied Chelsea's chest, along with her pierced nipples. Chelsea's body was more toned than Elizabeth's, but that did not create envy.

Fueling her sexual charge, she focused on Josh. His soft face was pale in the morning light as she looked into his sea-blue eyes, then down to his soft mustache and soul patch. His long blond hair ran down the length of his tattooed biceps. His soft shaved chest looked smooth. Elizabeth made her way to them, careful not to spill the contents of the plate. Once she stood at the foot of the bed, she placed down the plate and removed her robe. "Don't you look scrumptious?" she said as she crawled between them.

Chelsea and Josh curled up to her obediently.

"I hope you have your appetites, because Momma brought breakfast." Elizabeth separated herself from them as she crawled to the foot of the bed. After collecting the plate, she shuffled backward on her knees.

"That looks yummy," Chelsea remarked.

"It's the breakfast of champions," Josh added.

Elizabeth grabbed the twenty-dollar bill and rolled it into a tight cylinder. Josh grabbed the right side of the plate while Chelsea grabbed the left. In unison, they brought it to Elizabeth.

"You don't know what I had to go through to get this," Elizabeth said. "I had to give this grungy old fossil a free lap dance for this bean. It was actually kind of funny. Not funny *ha-ha*, but still funny. He wanted to take me back to his house for a private party. He told me he lives in that shitbag town Bradford, and if I ever want more bean, it's easy to get. It's plentiful there. All I really care about is having a solid hook-up," she said sourly as Chelsea keenly snorted her lines.

After Chelsea finished, she coughed and ran her fingers on the residual powder, followed by rubbing her gums, before passing the plate to Josh. "You've got to be kidding. He lives in Bradford? Isn't that the same town Seamus lives in?" Chelsea asked with a laugh.

Josh did his lines and coughed into painful laughter. "Wouldn't it be something if those two were neighbors? Hell, it's a small world."

"It wouldn't surprise me at all. I've already made that assumption. I'm not going to take the chance to find out. Seamus already keeps begging me to come over. That's all I need, to find out those two oafs live next to each other."

"Even though you talk shit about Seamus, you must admit, he did save you. If it wasn't for him, that redneck could have raped you—or worse," Chelsea said with concern.

Elizabeth locked eyes with Chelsea. "I'll give you that."

Josh turned from them, leaned over the bed, and slid the plate under.

"I was going to get screwed either way. I guess I was destined to have to fuck one of them. Honestly, I don't know what would've been worse. At least the redneck probably would've left me alone afterward. Seamus saved me one time and won't leave me alone. I admit I do fuck him on occasion, but something about him pleasantly surprised me." Elizabeth's eyes flared.

"Oh yeah, what's that?"

"Massive fucking cock. That boy is strapped in length and girth. When I ride that fucker, I feel like he's going to split me done the middle. Of course, that's the only way I can get off. He might be well endowed, but he doesn't know how to use it. Although it's fun while it last."

"You're one stone-cold bitch," Chelsea said with a depraved giggle, looked over Elizabeth's side, and saw Josh still leaning over. "Do you think he'd be interested in playing with both of us?"

Elizabeth's expression hardened. "Seamus wouldn't go for that. Despite me getting some pleasure from his huge cock, the guy freaks me out. He wants something I can't give him. He insists we're a couple and doesn't take the hint that I only occasionally want him."

Chelsea, however, still held intrigue.

Elizabeth knew she should crush Chelsea's curiosity and searched for the right words. "There's something about him you really wouldn't like. I don't like it either; in fact, I hate it."

Chelsea looked fearful, waiting for Elizabeth to finish.

Elizabeth had Chelsea right where she wanted. "Even if I could get past his ugly mug and I wanted something more, there's no way it could happen. Seamus is prejudice. After our third time together, I decided to test the water. I asked him what he felt about inviting another girl into the mix."

"What did he say?"

"He didn't like the idea one bit. He despises bi-girls. When he told me that, his face turned *really* scary. He became preachy, telling me about his past experiences. He said he'd been through that before. Seamus went on and on, saying a couple of previous girlfriends were bisexual and had cheated on him with their friends and their friend's boyfriends. He developed his own word for bi-girls."

"What does he call them?"

"Bi-hoes, as in whores."

"That's too bad. I would've liked to give that piece of pipe a try."

Josh shot upright and peered at both with hurtful eyes. He folded his arms and pouted. "What am I, chopped liver?"

Elizabeth and Chelsea snickered, each giving the other a false pout, before they pulled him between their bodies.

"Momma didn't mean to hurt your feelings. You have two things Seamus doesn't. You have looks and the ability to use your tongue in ways we could have never imagined," Elizabeth said.

Chelsea pampered his bruised ego as well. They made a move on each side of his neck, working their tongues.

His flaccid member grew.

Elizabeth worked her hand down, massaging him gently, raising him with each stroke.

Chelsea watched his member with disappointment. She only regarded it as average. Despite what Elizabeth had said about Seamus, Chelsea was still curious.

Elizabeth read Chelsea's expression and sternly nudged her.

Chelsea's curiosity broke, and she massaged Josh. Both moved in unison and licked his nipples.

Josh's face lightened as he tilted his head backward and sunk along the headboard until he lay flat.

They made their way down his torso, taking turns giving him oral pleasure.

"Did Chelsea and I fix you?" Elizabeth asked.

He grinned. "Oh yes, you did."

"I think one good turn deserves another." Elizabeth shifted her body between his and Chelsea's.

"I think I'd have to agree," Josh replied.

Elizabeth lay as Josh and Chelsea inched down, working their mouths as they parted each of her legs. They mixed and matched their tongues while Elizabeth grinned. *I'm one stone-cold bitch.*

Seamus flung the phone furiously to the passenger seat. He pulled through the parking lot onto Jenson Drive, fuming with rage, and accelerated onto Krotz Drive. Upon arriving at State Route 14, he didn't stop and was almost sideswiped. Seamus received a horn-cuss from the driver who almost struck him. In a reflex, Seamus flipped off the driver and continued eastbound.

"Fucking bitch! I've always been there when she needed. I fucking need her, and she's too busy. She's not too busy for her friends. Hell! I bet that trashy bi-hoe and Long Blonde Josh are already there!"

Despite his speed, Seamus felt he was traveling at a death crawl. Scenarios played in his mind. He considered three possible destinations. First, he considered going to Elizabeth's house to see if Josh's car was there. If it was, he was fearful of what he might do. Once he started on Josh, it would not end well, and Elizabeth would end their relationship forever.

The second possibility was to go to Hollow Grove. If he went there first, he would be close to Elizabeth's house. It would be the perfect excuse if he paid her a surprise visit. He could claim he was in the area, and it wouldn't be a lie. Seamus's mind returned to the possibility of Josh and Chelsea being at Elizabeth's house.

The third possibility placed him at home, avoiding contact with everyone. This option might be for the best. Carefully considering the third, he decided to avoid going to Elizabeth's home.

Seamus continued on State Route 14 until arriving at the intersection of Bradford Road. In a blind act, he made a left. Fear revisited as he questioned his motives. *Why the hell am I heading north?* Seamus strengthened his willpower and decided not to go any farther than Hollow Grove.

Seamus arrived at the intersection of Bradford and Hollow Ridge Road. He cut across the vacant parking lot toward the corner. The only vehicles present were his car and Mack's red Ford Bronco II.

I might as well pick up some beer for the weekend.

His car fell still as he turned off the engine. While passing the part of the fence with the missing boards, a memory popped. It was of the night he had met Elizabeth and what he had seen before entering the bar. Seamus poked his face through the gap. Oddly enough, everything he had seen that night was still there. The support tubes and the strange autoclave craft rested in broad daylight, only this time, a blue tarp covered the object, tethered by ropes tied to stakes in the ground.

He pressed his face deeper, hoping to get a better view in the natural daylight. The overgrown grass still obstructed his view. Seamus retracted his face and quickened his pace toward the cobblestone wall.

Regarding his memories further on the events of that night, he looked up toward the second-floor window, hoping to see the flashing lights. The lights were not present. Seamus resumed normal speed as he approached the entrance. With a firm grasp on the door handle, he opened it and entered.

Once his eyes adjusted, he became aware of two figures. Mack stood behind the bar, and a strange-looking man stood to the right. The unknown man was clad in attire Seamus could only describe as old-timey clothes—a three-piece suit, derby hat, and shoes with spats. Seamus listened as Mack and the stranger conversed.

"That sounds marvelous, Mr. McManaway. I think this will mutually benefit both of us." The stranger spoke with an old-time dialect.

"I'm glad to be a part of it, and I appreciate doing business with you." Mack shook the man's hand while smiling. Mack's smile broke when Seamus approached. "We should finish this conversation at another time, Roland. I have a customer."

"I concur," the strange man said before directing his attention toward Seamus. The stranger brushed shoulders with Seamus as they met in the middle. He studied Seamus while tilting his head. The man seemed to be making a long assessment while curling his mustache with his index finger.

Seamus fought the urge to laugh.

The stranger doffed his hat. "Good day, sir." His voice sounded a cross between a proper English accent and a New England accent—a Brahmin accent.

"Take it easy, bro," Seamus said as the stranger strode toward the entrance. Seamus faced Mack upon arriving at the bar, erupting into laughter. "What the fuck is up with Old Dapper Dan? This isn't the nineteenth century."

Mack's face hardened. "He and I have business, and I don't need you mucking it up."

"I'm chill, brother."

"If you're not chill, I'll bar you like I did Sweeney. Although I don't care; none of this will be my problem for long," Mack said, then followed up with an *Oh Shit* expression.

"What do you mean, 'None of this will be your problem for long?'"

"Nothing I just meant that if you get out of line, you'll be barred, and I won't have to worry about anymore scrapping. That's all I meant. Nothing more! What do you want?"

Seamus did not press his luck. He requested two cases of Busch Light.

Mack was eager to comply.

Seamus placed his money in Mack's hand and bid him a good day.

Mack halfheartedly acknowledged as Seamus made for the entrance.

When Seamus reached the corner of the cobblestone wall, he smelled something odd, like something synthetic was burning. As he walked, the smell changed into something he could not identify and became unnatural.

While hoping to identify the aroma, his gaze fell above the top of the fence. A dissipating vapor swirl of color moved above the fence line. The swirling represented the same colors that projected from the second-floor window. *White, green, purple, blue.* Seamus fell still as the powdery swirl disappeared. Something urged him to quicken his pace. Seamus already knew what he would see but still needed confirmation.

The strange object was gone. The supporting tubes were still present, and the tarp rested neatly and folded to the side, but the object was gone. Not wanting to remain any longer, he ran across the parking lot to his car. While driving, he did not think of anything but the road ahead. He had beer in his car, and if he did encounter anyone and told them about it, they would think he was crazy or drunk.

Something even more bizarre happened to him as he approached his neighborhood. His cases of beer spoke to him. *We'll be your only companions this Memorial Day Weekend. Oh, sure you can drink us and drown your sorrows, hell, maybe even catch a buzz, but just as soon as we're empty, you'll be empty. But don't worry. Unlike Elizabeth, we'll be around all weekend. See you soon.* Silence fell once again as Seamus turned left into the Wiley G. Estates.

Lynette Buckland came abruptly into view as she stood in the middle of Observation Drive.

Seamus stabbed his brakes as his car skidded to a stop. His body thrust forward then back. Instinctively, Seamus pounded his fist on his steering wheel.

Lynette nearly jumped out of her skin. After collecting herself, her fear-induced paralysis relinquished, and she moved from the center of the drive to the left side of the street.

Seamus pulled over his car to confront her.

Lynette stood in the moist grass, obediently awaiting his furious scolding, eyes glistening.

"What were you thinking, standing in the middle of the street? No one can see you if they are coming from that way." Seamus darted his hand passed her shoulder and pointed to the opening between the brick walls.

She turned, then refocused on him.

"People drive like fucking maniacs around here."

Lynette nodded without uttering a word.

Seamus realized he had made his point. He extended his hands, his palms opened, in a *calm down* motion.

Tears fell from Lynette's eyes.

Seamus relaxed and offered a warm smile. "I'm sorry. You just gave me one hell of a scare. You know how people drive around here. Most of these assholes learned to drive from watching *The Dukes of Hazard* and *The Fast and Furious* movies." Seamus laughed.

Lynette joined in with an opened-mouth smile. Her teeth and shiny, irritated acne repulsed Seamus.

Instead of displaying repulsion, he studied her figure and focused on her attire. His gaze fell just below her weak chin. She wore a sapphire-blue scoop neck belly top, adorned with sleazy leopard spots. He scanned farther down as he examined her exposed trim core. Her flesh appeared smooth and silky. It was quite the opposite of the oily flesh on her face. He surveyed her frayed high-rise booty shorts contouring tightly to her legs.

Lynette slid her right foot from her sandal and caressed the blades of grass with her big toe while swaying her hips in an *oh garsh* movement. She followed by batting her eyelashes at him, her eyes bright.

Seamus searched for something to say. "What were you doing in the middle of the street?"

Anticipation consumed Lynette as she glanced at her house, then eyed the entrance. Urgency gripped her as she retrieved her phone from her pocket. "I have a date with Todd," Lynette replied shamefully. She knew she should break if off with Todd and knew Seamus felt likewise. "Todd said he wanted to meet up. He swore it would be different. I told Dad I was going to hang out with Jenny. Besides, he wanted me out of the house because Travis is coming over. Please don't tell Dad."

Seamus winced while thinking about Jenny Shannon.

Lynette's eyes widened.

It was not his place to make any judgment, but Seamus knew Jenny's reputation. Jenny was the biggest whore in Bradford. Unfortunately, she was also Lynette's only friend who Greg would allow her see. This was likely because Greg took pleasure in ogling her.

Greg was nothing more than a hypocrite. He desired younger girls just as much as Todd did. Something about Jenny also reminded Seamus of Chelsea. Both seemed to be bad influences. In some ways, Seamus couldn't help to wonder if Jenny was the one who had set up Lynette with Todd, as if she was Lynette's pimp. Knowing Jenny and her reputation, she probably received a percentage.

Realizing his demeanor had soured, he conveyed a look of kindness, just as a random thought crossed his mind. He didn't know where it had come from, but he decided to go with it. Seamus employed reassurance before revealing his true intentions. "You don't have anything to worry about. I won't say shit to your old man. He and I are not exactly buddies. However, if you want my opinion, I think you should stay away from Todd. I've known him for a long time, and I know what he's about. You're a grown woman, and you can make your own decisions; it's really up to you." Seamus watched Lynette's body relax and assumed she was about to thank him. "I'm doing you a pretty big favor by keeping my mouth shut. I think one favor deserves another."

"Anything you want," she replied with desperation as she was drawn to the sound of Todd's truck approaching.

"Good. The time might come when I want something." Seamus wished her a good day.

While driving toward his house, he glanced in his mirrors and saw Lynette scurry out the entrance.

Todd gunned the accelerator to hurry her along.

Once Seamus parked, the sound of Todd's truck faded in the distance. Before grabbing his beer, he paused, wondering what kind of favor Lynette could offer and also where such a crazy idea had come from.

Greg Buckland and Travis Swisher chortled like a couple of idiots while standing on Greg's porch. Greg appeared to be in worse shape than he had earlier, and Travis looked as he normally did—clad in his thug-style attire. Greg halted his laughter when Seamus was within earshot.

Travis kept laughing, not realizing Seamus's presence. "Yeah, bro, if you ever need to score a bean, hit me up. I got you, a'ight?" Travis continued in his hood rat tone. "Just let me know if that sweet little thing wants a five or a ten next time. I got you, bro."

Greg tapped Travis across his chest with the back of his hand, then told him he'd call if he needed.

Travis strutted by Seamus, exhibiting swagger, greeting him with a "sup, dog."

Seamus bid him a rushed hello.

Travis asked Seamus if he wanted a bean to go with his beer.

Seamus declined. Upon entering his house, Seamus opened one of the cases and retrieved his first of many beers he would drink during the Memorial Day Weekend … alone.

CHAPTER 4
BETRAYAL AMONG FRIENDS

"Shut up." Seamus groaned while his phone rang. A terrible pain resided in his forehead. The previous days were a blur. What he remembered most was being glued to his recliner, watching the *Professor Phantasm Macabre Memorial Day Weekend Marathon.* Headache be damned, he sat upright to silence his phone. A dreadful boiled hotdog water taste greeted him. In an attempt to clear it, he forced a cough before grabbing his phone. "Hello?" he asked groggily.

"Is this Seamus Van Leer?" a cracked voice asked.

"What can I do for you?"

"This is Tina Oriber, JanStar site supervisor at Moline Medical Warehouse. I was wondering if you could start today."

"Start today?! I haven't had an interview yet."

"Your application was pressed through. We just had an employee walk out, so we need to fill the position ASAP. I'll have Bradley show you the ropes. After the shift ends, I'll give you an orientation."

"Okay, I'll get around."

"I'm looking forward to meeting you. Just sign in at the guardhouse. It's the little building to the right of the entrance. The guard will give you a guest badge. Bradley and I will be waiting for you in the cafeteria. Thank you for coming in."

"I'm looking forward to meeting you," Seamus said, not realizing Tina had hung up. "I bet she'll be a *real* dream to work for, the kind that turn into nightmares. I'll make the best of it until I find something better … I hope." Seamus grabbed an old t-shirt and tattered jeans. *What the hell did I get myself into? I can already tell the boss will be a bitch. Nevertheless, I really need this job. It's okay I won't be there long. I'll be out of sight and out of mind.* The strange thought echoed like a shooting shark. *A shooting shark? Don't I mean shooting star? What the hell is a shooting shark?* Seamus made for the front door.

Greg and Travis were standing next to Greg's minivan.

Seamus did not acknowledge them. However, their words captivated him as he discreetly listened while fumbling for his car keys.

"How'd it go with that stripper chick last night?" Travis asked.

"I got more than a lap dance."

"Did you fuck her?"

Greg glared and nudged Travis. "No, I didn't, but I got something almost as good."

"What could be almost as good?"

"It was kind of weird and cool at the same time.

"How could it be weird *and* cool?"

"I'm getting to that. I bartered with her for a private lap dance with the five. She turned me down and said her boss keeps a close eye. I wasn't about to give up, so I offered her a ten. She told me to hang out after the place closed so I could follow her home. I waited outside until her friend and her friend's boyfriend showed up. They told me I could watch them if I gave them the five and the ten. The only catch was I couldn't join."

"You got to watch two chicks get it on! What could've been weird about that?"

"The other bitch's boyfriend made it weird. It was cool watching the two sluts eat and toy each other, but when he got involved, it almost ruined it for me. I didn't want to see him. I just wanted to watch the whores. Although, after looking at his little prick and long blond hair, I would've sworn he was a bitch too."

Seamus froze after listening to Greg's description. It sounded like Josh. Seamus hoped Greg would elaborate more.

"That's fucked up, having to watch a dude in the mix. Where do these bitches live?"

Seamus couldn't linger; he needed to get to work, but he wanted—needed—to hear where this had happened, hoping Greg would absolve Elizabeth.

"They live north of here. I'm not exactly sure. I was pretty beaned up when I followed them. I think they took a couple extra turns to throw me off, but I remember the best parts. By the time they finished fucking, I bolted out. I don't even remember the drive home."

"Maybe next time they'll let you join. I'm bouncing out, bro," Travis said as he passed Seamus.

Seamus's mind reeled while he watched Greg enter his house. Seamus rammed his gearshift into Reverse and sped backward. He almost clipped Travis with the front of his car.

Travis shouted at Seamus as he sped away.

As Seamus drove along Observation Drive, he noticed Lynette standing by the entrance.

She smiled at him, but he didn't return the gesture.

The urge to intimidate Lynette crossed his mind. Seamus decided against it; he remembered his promise to her, along with his request of a favor. Besides, who really knew who Greg was talking about? There was no way to know for sure if it was Elizabeth. Seamus brooded as he drove through Bradford. Upon reaching Donaldson Road, he rationalized his thoughts. "That could've been anyone."

Upon arriving at State Route 14, his thoughts were comforting. *Greg was talking about some skanky bitch he met at the strip club. The nearest strip club is in Port Lucas. That's a big city. All sorts of freaks and perverts live there. It would be too crazy of a coincidence if it was Elizabeth, Josh, and Chelsea. I can't see Elizabeth working there.*

Calmness inhabited Seamus as he turned into the parking lot of Moline Medical Warehouse. Once he found a spot, he headed toward the guard shack.

"Can I help you, sir?" the guard asked.

"I'm Seamus Van Leer. This is my first day with JanStar." Seamus studied the guard. He couldn't put his finger on it, but he felt there was something familiar about the guard.

"Sign in on the clipboard. I'll let Tina know you're here."

Seamus glanced at the guard's nametag—Shawn V. After racking his brain, he could not place anybody by that name.

"I'll buzz you through. The cafeteria will be on your right." Shawn motioned.

"Thanks. I'll see you after work," Seamus said before walking toward the main building.

Seamus entered the cafeteria and saw two people sitting at the center table. Seamus walked confidentially to greet them.

A large woman stood with strained effort. The equally heavy-set man remained seated.

Seamus increased his speed; walking fast might prove to her that he was a motivated worker. He greeted her warmly, proffering his hand.

She returned the gesture and gave Seamus a toothless smile.

"I'm Seamus Van Leer."

"I'm Tina Oriber." She tapped the large man on his rounded shoulder. "This is my nephew, Brad Tipp. He'll be the one training you until you have a handle on things. Once you are comfortable, the three of us will comprise the dayshift team. We're glad to have you, aren't we, Bradley?"

"Pleased to meet you. Don't worry about that Bradley bullshit. Just call me Ox."

"Now that you two are acquainted, I'm going back to the office to make sure the paperwork is in order."

As Tina walked toward the doorway, Seamus noticed the similarities between Tina's looks and the singer/songwriter Paul Williams. Seamus almost burst with laughter as he now knew what an obese and toothless version of Swan from *Phantom of The Paradise* would look like.

"Don't let my aunt bullshit you. She's going to plant her ass and play on her phone." Ox laughed, exposing his black-holed gums.

"Shut your piehole. If your mother wasn't my sister, I'd have never hired your flabby ass." Tina howled playfully.

"Me and Aunt Tina like to talk trash. C'mon, I'll show you the ropes." Ox signaled for Seamus to follow. Ox pointed to the utility closet and informed Seamus that was where the shift sign in/out clipboard and the cleaning supplies were kept. Ox and Seamus reentered the cafeteria and walked to the warehouse floor.

The sound of heavy tow-motor traffic greeted them, as the warehouse associates were driving with little regard.

"You really need to watch your ass. These motherfuckers only care about making rate."

Although Seamus could not completely understand Ox, he gathered the strong points. *If you get in the way of a lift truck, pedestrian be damned.*

"We'll walk the perimeter. It's safer, and I can show you the locations of the trashcans."

They headed to the far-right corner of the facility and circumnavigated the perimeter. Ox took the lead as he watched for rogue tow-motors.

They walked single file per Ox's wishes. Dock door one hundred was the first door they passed. Seamus tried to pay close attention to Ox's instructions but had difficulty doing so. The back of Ox's shirt rode up while his pants slid down. Regardless, Seamus did his best to pay attention. Panic hit Seamus when they arrived at dock door one hundred three. Seamus held back a few steps once a familiar face from the past came into view.

Ox hollered an unremitting greeting at the tow-motor driver.

The driver stopped and waved modestly before setting his park brake.

Ox shuffled toward the driver while Seamus stayed back. It was Kenny Elnor.

Of all people, it would be the son of the people my parents killed.

Kenny politely waited for Ox, but it was clear he didn't want to be bothered.

"Hey, Ken-Ken! How's it going? You guys played a rocking show at Jeanelle's Bar!"

Kenny shielded his face from Ox's spraying words, clearly wanting to just return to work and not chitchat.

During the exchange, Ox gestured toward Seamus. "I'm training a new guy. I hope he works out. Aunt Tina told me all I had to do was drive the scrubbers and hopper trucks, and I didn't have to do the cleaning part anymore. That's why we have him."

Seamus turned from Kenny's line of sight, pretending to observe something in the facility while avoiding eye contact with Kenny.

Kenny bid Ox a polite farewell and returned to the trailer he was loading.

Ox signaled for Seamus to catch up, and they resumed walking. "That's my best friend Ken-Ken. He plays in a band called Lapis Lazuli. I was the one who started it. They wanted me on lead vocals, but I was cool with being manager instead. I enjoyed doing it, but I never got along with the bass player. He's a cocky prick. I think the other band members are getting tired of his shit. Maybe if they get rid of him, I can go back to being their manager." Ox pointed to a small structure at the center of the warehouse and explained they weren't allowed to enter.

Seamus observed a large, unpleasant man yelling at a timid woman sitting in front of a computer.

Ox led Seamus to the opposite side of the structure where the restrooms were located and informed Seamus of the rest of cleaning schedule. They continued until the tour ended at dock door one hundred seventy.

Seamus was satisfied with his knowledge of the facility. At 1:30 p.m., Ox and Seamus reported to the utility closet.

Tina sat behind her cluttered desk.

Seamus sat in a rickety office chair in front of Tina's desk.

Ox grew restless as he stood in the doorway. "Can you sign me out?"

"Did you get everything done today?" Tina asked.

"Yeah, we worked hard."

"Okay, get out of her and tell my sister that she should be ashamed for cursing me with a nephew like you."

"Okay, Aunt Tina. I hope you're coming over for the cookout this weekend."

"I'll be there as long as you don't eat everything. Get out before I make you work a double."

Ox made his way like a runaway train while Tina laughed.

"Oh, boy, my nephew is something else. He's a bit of a bullshitter and not the brightest bulb, but he knows his job. Frankly, I don't think anyone else would've hired him. I want to warn you; he tries to delegate his work onto others." She redirected her tone before speaking again. "Do you think this job is something you'd be interested in doing?"

"I think so."

"Good. Here is your employee handbook. Inside, you'll find our operating procedures and our drug and alcohol policy." Tina leaned forward in a clandestine manner. "First, I'll tell you about signing in and out. You need to be here at least five minutes before the beginning of your shift. I'm always in here around one thirty every afternoon. I don't really mind if you leave early, but I'd rather you leave only ten to fifteen minutes if you do. The only reason I let Ox go early was I didn't want his mother claiming that I worked him too hard. If, for any reason, you want to duck out early, I'll mark you out at two o'clock. It gives you a chance to beat the afternoon rush. One more thing before I let you go. Did you realize we didn't require a drug test?" Tina whispered.

"Yes."

"You don't have to read it, but I want you to understand how our drug and alcohol policy works. I'm not stupid. I know most people work for us because it's an easy job, but the other reason is because we don't drug test. I don't care what you do. You can smoke all the dope you want, but if you get in an accident, the company will require you to undergo a drug test. If it comes back positive, I'll have to let you go."

"I drink sometimes, but you don't have to worry."

"That's not any of my business. Go ahead and sign out and have a good afternoon. I'll see you tomorrow." Tina proffered a meaty handshake.

Seamus left the makeshift office into the afternoon sunlight.

Shawn stood outside the side door of the guard shack, smoking a cigarette. He jumped when Seamus came into view.

Seamus reassured him it would be all right if he finished his smoke.

Shawn stepped in and held open the door. "I finished your entry badge. I just need to get a picture for your JanStar badge."

"I think you need to turn on the light. It's too dark in here."

"Okay, stand against the wall." Shawn took Seamus's picture, ejected the SD card from the camera, and placed it inside the computer drive. "I'll have both badges ready tomorrow."

Seamus sensed Shawn's unease. "Sorry about staring. You look familiar, but I can't place it.

"You'd be surprised how many times I hear that. If I had a dollar for every time, I could quit this job and follow my passion."

"What's your passion?"

"I want to be a novelist. I've been tinkering around with this crazy idea about a guy meeting some alien woman from a distant place in time or some alternate universe, but I haven't decided her origin."

"It sounds like a decent story," Seamus said before an awkward silence settled. "I'll see you tomorrow." Seamus stepped out.

"I'll be present and accounted for," Shawn said grimly.

I know that dude from somewhere. I'm sure of it. Seamus fastened his seatbelt, and his phone rang. "Hello?"

"Hi, hero. What's up?"

"I just got off work."

"I was just thinking about you."

"I'm always thinking about you. I wished I could've seen you last weekend."

Elizabeth cringed at the thought of being stuck with Seamus, especially since that grubby guy she had scored beans from might live close to him. "I know, babe, but Chelsea and Josh needed me."

Seamus mouthed silent curses.

Elizabeth enjoyed Seamus's jealousy. "Are you there?"

"I'm here, honey. My signal must have gotten weak. I'm glad to hear from you. I can't get you out of my head."

Elizabeth heard all she needed. "So, you've missed me?"

"Yes. I think about you all the time. I need you."

"I need a ride to the Port Lucas Mall for some new clothes. There's a store that has exactly what I need."

Surprise, surprise, she needs something.

Elizabeth sensed Seamus's negativity and decided she would employ her best method of motivation. "C'mon, babe. You know it's been a while since we've seen each other. I have other needs too. God! I haven't been able to think of anything else but your huge cock," Elizabeth said while faking an orgasm.

"I'll go home and grab a change of clothes."

"Don't bother. Just get your ass up here. I miss you so much." Elizabeth ended the call. The last thing she wanted was to hear that he loved her. When he had said he missed her, it made her feel uncomfortable enough, but to have heard *love* would have really grossed her out.

I'm glad she hung up. I probably would've freaked her out if she heard me say I love her. Seamus exited the parking lot with raring speed.

His heart thumped so hard he felt it in his throat. Although he could not see his own reflection, he felt his eyes were projecting stars as he hurriedly placed his car into Park. He flew up the steps of the side entrance and walked through the door without thinking to knock.

Elizabeth stepped from the kitchen and startled when she saw him. Elizabeth was a sight to behold, wearing a white tank top that exposed her cleavage, along with sporting black high-rise short shorts, and black sandals with the ankle clasps.

"Are you ready?"

"Yeah, honey, let's get to that store." Elizabeth passed Seamus with force.

Seamus followed her and opened the passenger door.

Elizabeth rode in silence. When they arrived at the Port Lucas Mall, Elizabeth stepped out quickly and strode toward the Dillard's entrance.

Seamus quickened his pace to keep up.

They entered the foyer, and she distanced herself from him as they strolled through women's casual.

Is she ashamed of me? Seamus fell back a few steps.

Once they entered the mall, they passed a couple staple stores before arriving at Rachel's Taboo Boutique. Elizabeth stood at the entrance and turned to Seamus while he stared at the overhead marquee.

Seamus felt apprehension as he remembered Greg and Travis's conversation. The hot-pink cursive signage of the word *Rachel* did not bother him, but it was the letter *T* in *Taboo* that made him uneasy. It had a silhouette of an exotic dancer arching backward while her hair dipped to the ground. The silhouette of the dancer had her leg wrapped around the stem of the letter like a stripper pole. Seamus wanted to keep his poker face and brought his gaze forward.

"Are you coming?"

"I never knew a store like this existed. I guess I don't make it up here often."

Elizabeth extended her hand.

Seamus felt light as a feather as he joined her, but his suspicion returned as Elizabeth seemed to know the layout.

Elizabeth started with the shoe section and selected a clear pair of spiked stilettos—the smuttiest shoes Seamus had ever seen. She went to the skirts and selected a neon-green mesh mini skirt. She sashayed toward the bras and grabbed a skimpy bra that was the same color as the mini skirt. It looked like it would barely cover her nipples. She turned and asked him if he was ready to go.

Masking his discomfort, he asked if she wanted to try on the items. *Has she been here before?* His suspicions increased when the overly made-up blonde cashier seemed to recognize her.

Elizabeth removed large bills from her pocket while sensing his suspicion. "I've been so excited to model this stuff for you."

"How do you know they'll fit? You didn't try them on."

"Babe, most of these clothes goes by one size fits most, and besides, if it's a little small, it'll reveal more of me for you to see." Elizabeth made a valid point. With all the stuff in her wardrobe, she probably already had a good idea of her size. Elizabeth led him through the mall to his car.

Once at home, Elizabeth carried the items close to her body as she ran through her house.

Seamus was quick to keep up.

As she cleared the last step of the second floor, she increased her speed and closed the door in his face.

Seamus stewed with frustration for a moment. He raised his hand to pound the door, but the door flung open.

Elizabeth stood adorned with the new items. The attire was too small for her just as she had predicted.

Seamus grew hard with a pulsing erection.

Elizabeth pushed him on the bed and pulled off his clothes. She rode him until she achieved ecstasy. They both arrived together on her last climax.

Seamus lay in the blissful throes of orgasm. The moment was not held long; shortly after, Elizabeth urged him to get dressed.

She ushered Seamus down the stairs.

Seamus attempted to procrastinate but complied. He made one last attempt as they entered her kitchen. "I don't want to leave." He pulled his phone from his pocket. "It's five forty-five. We have plenty of time."

"You know you have to wake up early. I want to ensure you make it home safe so you can come back and give it to me again. You don't want to get in a wreck, do you?"

"I guess not."

"I thought you'd agree. You know I'd miss you if anything happened." She responded flirtatiously.

Seamus wanted nothing more than to tell her he loved her. Instead, he leaned in for a kiss. To his surprise, she returned the kiss. Seamus floated like a feather as he strode to his car.

Even the typical dread he felt when he entered Bradford didn't seem as harsh. For once, he felt impervious to the place.

Even Observation Drive felt smoother under his wheels. By the time he reached his porch, he felt twenty pounds lighter. A rewarding night's sleep was imminent.

Seamus did, in fact, rest well. His dreams were vague and nonsensical. Despite the vagueness, he remembered the last part—an outline of a multi-colored shark, illuminated with the same color patterns he had seen from the second-floor window of Hollow Grove and in the vapor swirl from the rear of the bar on the day he had seen Mack with the stranger. The unusual shark crossed his eyes like a shooting star. As it finished passing, he woke up wide eyed.

He stepped from his bed and took a refreshing shower. Seamus wished Elizabeth was with him. The thought aroused him, but he expelled it; he did not have time for self-gratification. He finished his shower, dressed, and left his house.

The duration of the week was pleasantly uneventful. Seamus reported to work, and Ox showed him the ropes. Each day that passed, Seamus exhibited more independence. At the end of each day, he tried to call or text Elizabeth.

She never answered the phone; instead, she only texted him single-word responses.

While Seamus was disappointed, he was not all together heartbroken. When Thursday arrived, he concluded training and was turned loose. Seamus realized what Tina had meant earlier about Ox. Just as she had predicted, Ox delegated more duties upon Seamus.

When Friday arrived, he was excited for the weekend and the possibilities that lay ahead. He was unsure whether he would see Elizabeth but hoped he would. If he could not see her, he would relax and drink. Maybe instead of drinking at home, he would go to Hollow Grove or keep it local and go to Maxwell's Bar and Grill. Either way, he had options.

Seamus checked his phone—11:00 a.m. It was time to clean the cafeteria. He collected his cleaning items and filled a mop bucket in the sanitation office. He entered the cafeteria, and his heart sank as he saw four people at the center table.

Kenny Elnor sat with two other men, while Ox stood next to them, attempting to join their conversation. Kenny tried to be polite to Ox, but the others were rude.

"Are you guys playing this weekend?" Ox asked as they ignored him.

Seamus manuevered to the other side of the room unnoticed.

"I'd love to party down," Ox continued.

One of Kenny's companions, a gawky-looking guy, turned to Ox. "Yeah, Ox, we have a show, and it's *veeeeerrry* far away. I don't know how you'll get there. Your mom might get lost taking you." He nudged Kenny.

Kenny brushed him off and glared.

"I don't need my mom to take me."

Kenny's other companion, a well-dressed, balding guy, displayed a sharp look. "We really need to talk about this, Kenny. All of us want your opinion."

The subject made Kenny feel uneasy. It didn't help matters either that Ox kept blithering on. Through his building annoyance, Kenny spoke. "Hey, Ox, we have some important band stuff to discuss."

"Okay, Ken-Ken," Ox said, realizing his welcome had been overstayed.

The gawky guy hollered as Ox passed through the double doors, "Have a nice day, Ox!"

Kenny backhanded him. "He's a little slow. Can't you show compassion? I think it should be Alex, Nik, and me having this meeting about you, instead of us having it about Nik. Let's get this over with. I hate taking a late lunch, and I don't feel right about talking about a friend."

"I'm not saying we can't still be friends with him, but he's not a good fit anymore," the balding man said. "It's like Desi said, we need to stop playing that progressive-rock shit and go back to the basics. An audience wants to party and not see a bunch of showboating assholes."

"That's a fine suggestion. Why don't we listen to what Desi has to say? She despises us and hates you being in the band."

"I hate to admit it, but Kenny has a *helluva* point," the gawky man said.

"Shut the fuck up, Andy. This isn't about Desi; it's about the future of our band. Besides, aren't you getting tired of him getting all the attention? I mean, I'm happy with Desi, but I know you guys wouldn't mind having a shot at some of the wildlife," Alex said as Kenny stood.

"I've got to get back to work. If you guys want to mention these issues to Nik, go ahead. I really don't want to be a part of this." Kenny left the table, headed for the warehouse.

Alex's frustration grew as Kenny approached the exit. "You know damn well this conversation isn't over! After we're done with the Westor Rapids show, we're having a meeting at my place. Nik won't be part of it, and if you decide you're not coming, consider yourself out! Nik might have been the one who started this, but I'm the one who hosts the practices! It would be in your best interest to show up!"

"Okay, Big Shot, I'll be there. I think it's shitty, but I'll be there!"

Alex and Andy sat quietly before leaving. They looked at Seamus, baffled they hadn't noticed him earlier.

Seamus returned to his task. *I feel bad for this Nik guy.* He contemplated his own situation. As much as he loved Elizabeth, he couldn't help but to consider the writing on the wall. At ten till noon, he finished the cafeteria.

During the rest of the day, he checked the bathrooms throughout the warehouse and the dock door trash. It was a quarter till two when Seamus headed to the sanitation office. "I'd like to sign out now."

"That's probably a good idea. Everyone is going to be acting like mad dogs getting out of here," Tina said as Seamus remained disconnected. "Are you okay?"

"I'm just ready to go."

"Have a good day."

Seamus turned from the utility closet and left work. *If these guys can betray a friend so easily, I wonder how easily a lover could betray the other.*

Chapter 5
Ross's Revelation

Seamus was not the only one with thoughts of betrayal. A couple of towns over, another man struggled with similar thoughts. Ross sat on his recliner and placed his bowl of pretzels on the remote stand. The living room was still; a soft glow of light shined through the windows. Ross grabbed his remote and aimed it at the TV. Before he turned it on, he looked around and praised himself on his possessions. His smile widened as he cherished everything he owned, especially his queen. Days like these were the best. There was no work scheduled, and he could sit in his castle all day. Just as his favorite fishing show started, a clandestine voice came from down the hallway. Suspicion's icy finger scraped his spine.

Ross leaned toward the hallway, hoping to hear the conversation between his wife and whoever she was talking to. It was times like these that made him hate her. Before he married Samantha, he had been in an unhappy marriage. His infidelity with Samantha had been the cause of his divorce. However, Ross never blamed Samantha. If it wouldn't have been for meeting her at the Sandousten Classic Car and Bike Festival and having the affair, it would have been something else that caused his divorce. But what he had with Samantha was different. Ross loved her and provided her with a good life—a life some young punk could never offer. She would be foolish to betray him.

Ross collapsed deeper into his recliner and increased the TV's volume to add to the guise that he was not eavesdropping.

Samantha peeked through the cracked bedroom door as she talked to her sister. She listened closely for any sounds that would tip her off. Unknown to Ross, Samantha was packing an overnight bag. "I think I can talk freely. It sounds like he's engrossed in his dumbass show." Samantha placed her most appealing piece of lingerie in her bag. "Girl, I don't know what you see in the fat bastard. I can't imagine what goes through your mind when you let him fuck you."

Samantha smiled devilishly. "I think about his money every time he gets that little Q-tip dick hard."

"Does that work? You still have to look at him and feel his nasty hands.""There's something else that helps." Samantha's body tingled all over.

"What's that?"

"I think of Nik and our night together. Last night, Ross wanted some, and I wasn't in the mood. I was so fucking disgusted with him, so I dove into my memories, and something strange happened."

"What happened?"

"I had an orgasm. I'd like to say it was the best sex I'd ever had with Ross, but that would be a lie. There's no such thing as good sex with Ross."

"That Nik guy must have thrown you a good one, if just thinking about him could get you off."

"Ever since our night together, it's all I crave."

"Wow, he sounds intense."

"I didn't tell you the best part."

"What's the best part?"

"The best part was Ross's reaction. He was more surprised than me. At first, he was feeling sure of himself. 'Oh, babe, was it as good for you as it was for me?' I just kept my eyes closed. After I opened my eyes, I must have made a face. It was like he could tell I was fantasizing about someone else. I had to reassure Ross that it was all because of him. Eventually, he bought it, rolled over, and fell asleep. I stayed awake and listened to him fart and snore. I thought about something before I fell asleep. This is where you come in. I want to come over. I know I'm putting you in a hard place, but I want to hopefully see Nik."

"I'm worried about you getting caught. What if Ross decides to investigate further?"

"I'm ready to take my chances. I know it sounds crazy, but I think I'm falling for Nik. I know he doesn't have Ross's money, but I think I'd be happier. Besides, he is *sooo* fucking hot, and he's closer to my age. Nik might have feelings for me too. I tested him before I bolted."

"What did you do?"

"I threw him the *I love you* sign, and he waved it back."

"I'd be lying if I said you shouldn't break your vows, but the truth is I can't stand Ross. It's disgusting that he wants to possess you. Come over. Hopefully, you can get a real man."

"You're the best sister in the world. I'll talk to you later. Goodbye." Samantha ended the call and zipped her overnight bag. She strode down the hallway into the living room. Samantha eyed Ross with disgust; he resembled a pile of manure. "I want to see Miranda and the baby," Samantha said while pacing the elongated living room.

"The last time you were there, you were acting weird when I picked you up." Ross reached for his bowl of pretzels and beer and placed the bowl on his lap.

"Fine! If you're too busy, I'll ask Darius," Samantha said, knowing she would get a reaction.

Ross was a racist and showed no effort to conceal it. He believed Darius decreased the property values on Tiffin Street and was likely a drug dealer. Ross also knew Darius had a thing for Samantha. On numerous occasions, when Samantha laid out in the front yard, Darius would pull over his Cadillac and approach Samantha. Darius would ogle her, and it drove Ross to murderous rage. Ross would storm out and demand she go inside. Accusations and threats would fly as soon as they entered the house. Darius would always give Ross a cocky smile that said, *I'm going to tap your wife sooner rather than later.*

"If Darius ever steps one foot inside, I'll shoot him, and I'd have the right to do so."

Ross also accused Samantha of wanting Darius. Ross insisted that was why she laid out in the front yard instead of the back. Samantha claimed she got the best sunlight in the front. This argument seemed to be happening more often. Each time it did, Ross grew closer to violence.

Ross stood and knocked over his bowl. "There's no way in hell you're going anywhere with him! I don't like the way he looks at you, and I especially don't like the way you act around him! You're my wife, dammit. You need to remember that!" Ross quivered with fury.

One way or another, she was leaving.

"Get your shit packed! I'll take you myself! Stay the fuck away from Darius, or you'll be out on your ass!" He sized up his wife. She wore one of her sexiest outfits. Her scantily clad body drove him further into a jealousy.

She started to walk away but was stopped when he grabbed her arm.

"If I ever catch you talking to Darius again, you'll pay dearly," Ross hissed.

"Are we done?"

"If I ever catch him in my house, I'll shoot his ass and yours! The police will believe me when I tell them my beautiful wife was the casualty of a horrible accident."

Samantha normally felt contempt for Ross, but now she was terrified. If Ross couldn't have her, no one would. Getting away meant everything. She dashed down the hallway and collected her bag.

The sudden urge to vomit struck Ross. He wiped his forehead with his meaty hands.

Samantha returned with her bag in tow.

Ross was flabbergasted to see she was already packed. He wanted to question her but suppressed the impulse. Instead, he employed a calmer tone. "Are you ready to go?"

"Obviously."

Ross and Samantha left in silence as she marched toward his truck. Ross walked casually, hoping his neighbors would not notice, especially Darius. The thought of him taking advantage of the situation made him seethe. Ross fought for coolness. The trip to Gibbswood was met with unsympathetic silence.

Samantha became antsy as they entered the village.

Sickness returned to Ross. Unable to control it, he let loose with a nervous belch.

Upon pulling up to Sattler Street, Samantha sprung from her seat and collected her bag.

Ross had to stab his brakes to stop. If he would not have stopped, he might have run her over with his back tires. "Hold your horses. I could've run you over!"

"I'm sure you would've made it look like an accident."

"I deserved that, and I'm sorry."

"Bye!" Samantha said curtly, slammed the door, and approached Miranda's porch.

Miranda and Troy stared callously at Ross.

As Ross pulled away, he saw Miranda and Troy waving their fists and cussing.

Troy puffed his chest, while Miranda rocked her free fist at Ross before passing her baby to Samantha. Miranda ran off the porch and gave Ross a double-barreled flip off.

Ross diverted his eyes and concentrated on the road ahead.

"I'm glad to be away from him," Samantha said as she handed Miranda her baby.

"I don't see how you put up with him," Miranda responded, soothing her fussy baby.

"I haven't been able to stand him for the longest time." The wheels in her head spun. "Ross threatened me before we got here."

"He did what? Troy! Go inside and lay the baby down."

"Fine, but I want to hear about this."

Miranda and Samantha stood silent, each smoking a cigarette while waiting for Troy to return.

"What did he say?" Troy demanded as Miranda offered him a cigarette. Troy turned the bill of his black cap backward and flexed his tattooed chest.

Samantha stole a look before refocusing on Miranda with a pitiful expression. "It started because of my neighbor Darius. You know Ross is incredibly racist."

Miranda and Troy agreed. "That dumb motherfucker is going to get his ass killed," Troy added.

Miranda shot him a sharp look.

Troy stepped backward.

"I told Ross I wanted to come over while he was watching his boring fishing show. He didn't want to be bothered and said something like I had already been over and that I was acting weird when he picked me up. You all know why I was acting weird. I had just gotten back in the nick of time before he got here. Ha! Nick of time—Nik! No pun intended." Samantha laughed. "Ross didn't want to take me, so I suggested Darius would."

"I bet that went well," Miranda said.

"It didn't. You know I'm not into black dudes; I'm not a racist like Ross, but I'm just not into them. I know Darius has a thing for me, but I would never be with him, although I'd never say that to Ross. But that's not the point. Ross said something that scared me. He said if he ever caught me talking to Darius, he would beat me, and, worse yet, if he ever caught Darius in the house, he would shoot him and me and make it look like an accident. He threatened my fucking life!"

"He did what?" Troy angrily punched the porch column.

Samantha and Miranda jumped.

"It's fucking on now! Get in the house!" Troy stormed through the front doorway as Miranda and Samantha followed. Troy directed Samantha and Miranda to sit while they scurried to the couch. "I need you to be completely honest!"

Samantha tried to answer, but her throat closed. Flooding tears fell from her eyes.

Miranda comforted Samantha and watched Troy with terror. "What the fuck is wrong with you?"

"I'm sorry. I just go crazy when a man treats a woman like that. I don't tolerate any motherfucker being violent to a woman." Troy approached Samantha as she held her face in her hands. He gently pried away her hands. "When I was five years old, my father walked out on me and my mom. It was hard, but we managed. About the time I turned eight, my mother met Dan while waitressing. Dan immediately disliked me, and he'd skin my ass daily. My mother would try to defend me, but that only made things worse. When I was ten, I was hanging out in my room one night when Dan came home drunk. My mom didn't have the house cleaned to his liking and went after her. All I could do was lie in my bed and cry. I cried like a baby as I listened to him beat her in the kitchen. I fucking lost it and raced from my bedroom to theirs. I knew the bastard kept a 9mm under the bed. I grabbed it and raced down the hallway. At first, I wanted to scare him, but by the time I got to the kitchen, I saw my mom sitting on the floor, a bloody mess. I blacked out and took a chance. I aimed and pulled the trigger. I got that prick right in the head." Troy struck his head to illustrate. "I put the motherfucker down. Our neighbors must have heard the shot and called the police. I was my mother's hero. She was hospitalized for a while, and I stayed at my grandmother's house. I'm sure if I hadn't stopped Dan, he would have killed her. "If you ever want Ross done, all you have to do is say the word. I will take care of him, permanently."

Samantha's bright, heterochromia eyes sparkled.

A feeling flashed through Troy as he watched her. He had always found Samantha attractive and often thought if he hadn't hooked up with Miranda, he would have tried for Samantha.

Before Troy could react, Samantha lunged at him and wrapped her arms around him.

Troy returned the embrace as Samantha cried into his bare shoulder.

Miranda beamed at Troy with jealousy.

Troy retreated quickly and walked to the front door to watch the afternoon horizon.

Miranda went to Samantha to console her.

Unknown to Miranda, Samantha and Troy shared another look.

Ross wanted to double back and survey Miranda's house after he cleared Sattler Street. Instead of following through, he decided to pull over and collect himself. Ross parked his truck in front of Jeanelle's Bar.

A few cars passed as he stood by the driver's side door. After checking the traffic, he rushed across the street to escape the afternoon heat. His breaths heaved as he reached the front door. After slowing his breathing, he entered the air-conditioned bar. His sweat felt like freezing rain. *Man, I can't believe I'm in this bad of shape.* Ross took labored steps toward the corner of the bar.

An attractive woman closer to his own age captivated him. She approached with a welcoming smile as she made her way from behind the bar. "What can I get for you?"

Ross almost said her phone number. "A bottle of Budweiser would be fine."

"Okay, coming right up."

Ross studied her body, as a man joined her from behind the bar counter.

Before leaving, the man grabbed the woman and affectionately kissed her.

The woman returned the kiss.

I wish me and Samantha were like that.

The bartender approached Ross while he scrambled to shake himself from his daydream.

Desperately, he looked for any means of distraction and spotted a bulletin board hung to his left containing the bar menu and current specials. Ross read it as if he were studying for a test. His glance shifted to the side of the bulletin board, where a white posterboard featured a collage of photographs of a band playing live. At the top of the poster were the words *Memorial Day Weekend Party*. Ross eyed it absently before his attention was redrawn to the bartender.

"Those guys played one hell of a show," she said.

"It looks like it was a good time. I wish I could've been here."

"They call themselves Lapis Lazuli. Charlie and I want to have them back. It was a good time, and it made us some extra money. I was skeptical at first, because they seemed a little progressive, but they proved to be a great act."

Ross smiled, and as he raised the bottle, he glanced again, then nearly purged his beer onto the bartender. His throat screamed with sharp, carbonated pain as he stood to accommodate the swallow. He couldn't believe his eyes. The picture under the black-scrolled letters revealed the back of his wife at the front of the stage. Ross would recognize her backside anywhere. Samantha had been in town the other weekend but had said she didn't go anywhere. At first, he tried to employ denial. *I'm not positive that's Samantha.* Sickness groped him as the poster beckoned him. Reluctantly, he looked again.

Ross saw another damning picture that exhausted his denial. The picture revealed Samantha ogling the leader of the band with stars in her eyes. Envy drenched Ross; he went into autopilot as he fetched his wallet.

"Are you ready to close out your tab?" the bartender asked. "Are you feeling okay, sir?"

Ross didn't reply. He turned slowly and left. He didn't feel the change in temperature from the cool air to the oppressing heat. He shambled to his truck without checking traffic. Without any memory of the events, he drove home. The pictures in the bar were all he could see.

Solace was not found that evening as he watched television, drank beer, and ate pretzels. His eyes felt heavy while daylight escaped. He dipped his head drowsily as fatigue enslaved him. As his head drooped, his phone rattled him awake. The pretzel bowl resting on his lap toppled. "Dammit, that's the second time today!" He answered the phone.

"Hi, Uncle Ross, it's your favorite niece, Desi. I hope I didn't get you at a bad time."

"Why are you calling me so late?" Ross adjusted his eyes and focused on the time—10:15 p.m.

"I have something important to tell you, and I hope you're sitting down."

Ross shifted to the edge of his recliner. *Can you spare the dramatics? I'm literally sitting on the edge of my seat.*

"This isn't easy to say, but you deserve to know. Samantha cheated on you the other night, and I know the person she did it with."

Ross's heart sank. "How can you be sure? I can't deny I've had suspicions, but how do you know?"

"My boyfriend told me. He's in a band with the guy she did it with. His name is Nik Vanelli."

At once Ross knew who he was. "When did this happen, and are you sure it was Samantha?"

"It happened on Memorial Day weekend after Alex's band played at this bar in Gibbswood. Alex told me that his co-partner hooked up with a girl from the audience. That pretty boy sonofabitch practices at our place in the poll barn. The other weekend, Alex had the band over, and I got into an argument with them, because they took time away from me and Alex. Despite them always insulting me, I was nice to them. I even bought them pizza."

Ross rolled his eyes. "I'm sorry to hear that, but I still don't see how this proves it was Samantha."

"After we sat down to eat, the other guys started picking on me, and things got heated. Alex stormed out and chewed their heads off. When he came back inside, he was still pissed off. Alex went on and on the rest of the day. As a good girlfriend, I let him vent. Alex complained the most about Nik. Alex claims he and Nik are good partners musically, but, in truth, he despises him. This led to something else; he said Nik was bragging about a conquest he'd had after the Gibbswood show. Nik gave Alex a detailed story about what he did with the girl. Nik told Alex that her name was Samantha. It was your Samantha, Uncle Ross, and I have irrefutable proof."

"What's that, Desi?"

"Nik said something about her strange eyes. He said she had one green eye and one blue eye. That cuts it right there. There aren't too many people running around with two different-colored eyes. I'm sorry you had to hear this, but you deserve to know."

Ross sat as the images from earlier inundated his mind. "I've got to go, Desi."

"If you need anything, just give me a call. Even though you're not married to my aunt anymore, you'll always be Uncle Ross."

Ross ended the call without saying goodbye. He placed his phone into his pocket and walked to his bedroom. He stripped to his underwear and crawled under the covers. His mind played numerous scenarios of what Samantha and Nik had done.

Pain and chaos plagued Ross as he stirred in a black void. There were no definable barriers, but he saw something in the distance that resembled a doorway. In this realm, he could walk and move faster than he could in the real world. *Am I dreaming? I never dream.* He stepped into the threshold and saw someone's bedroom. After looking around, he tried to enter, but his feet were frozen. He looked down, realizing he was dressed in his clothes from earlier that day. The longer he stood, the interior of the bedroom gained clarity. *What's going on?* he thought while hanging in the midst of two realities.

A presence passed through him. Ross saw the back of an athletic man with the silky legs of a woman wrapped around his torso. The man tossed the woman on his bed and undressed in front of her. The man was completely erect. Jealousy crawled over Ross as he diverted his glance from the man's size and concentrated on the woman who was still gaining clarity—Samantha.

Ross tried to lunge and stop them, but his body grew heavy. Ross helplessly watched the man retrieve a condom from his nightstand—a Magnum. Rage and pain devoured Ross. It became maddening as he watched helplessly as the man delivered his wife with vitality. The ecstasy on her face heightened his torment. Ross had never seen such a look of pleasure on her. No longer able to tolerate it, Ross begged for release.

After making his plea, the man and his wife stopped and directed their attention to Ross. Samantha cackled and gave him a wiggled finger wave. The man gave Ross a thumbs up, raised his left arm, and flexed his defined bicep before grabbing the backs of Samantha's ankles.

Ross no longer pleaded for release. All he wanted was to rush and kill them. They deserved to die, especially after antagonizing him. Ross's body gained mobility as his legs loosened. His hands tightened into hard fists. He placed a heavy foot inside the bedroom but was stopped before he could advance.

A cold hand pinched Ross's shoulder as the bedroom vanished. Ross spun with pulling force. The black void surrounded him again. With scrambling fear, he looked around and could not locate the doorway; it had vanished. Fear lay that he would never return home.

As sound crawled from his throat, a voice commanded him to stop. "Shut up! You're acting childish, my good man." The voice spoke in a strange accent. It sounded like a blend between a posh English accent and a New England accent—a Brahmin accent? *How do I know what kind of accent that is?*

"Who goes there? Answer me now, goddammit!"

"Taking the Lord's name in vain is not becoming. It's especially not becoming of a godless bag of bile like you. For the present moment, I mean you no harm. I only mean to enlighten you and offer you service. However, if you continue to act in such a manner, I'll provide you an abundance of harm."

Ross grew still.

"It richly pleases me that you're smarter than you appear. Although I would have enjoyed inflicting pain, I'd rather offer you help. We have much use for you."

"Who in the hell are *we*?"

"Right you are, my good man, right you are. Please let me illuminate you."

A snap echoed in the blackness. Ross's body returned to a natural state, and the hollow ground under him hardened. He was standing on a smooth surface. He turned to watch the overhead lights blink on in progression. The lights looked like chandeliers. The waves continued until the room came into view. It wasn't a regular room; it was some sort of dancehall. It looked monochromatic, like the ones in the classic black and white films. Eventually, color manifested from the top to bottom.

People also started to inhabit the place. At first, they were blurred blotches, but then, like Ross, they gained structure. They engaged in activities, as if they were in mid act. The men and women matched the appearance of the setting as they were dressed like flappers and sheiks. The people danced while a jazz band played.

Ross couldn't believe what he was seeing; it was just like the speakeasy scenes in the movies he had watched as a kid. The band looked authentic as the horn section played. There was even a colored guy in the right corner of the stage playing an ivory piano. A cigarette girl brushed into Ross and offered him some Lucky Strikes. He declined.

"Not really dressed for the occasion, are you, sugar?" She asked, sounding like Betty Boop.

Ross smiled at her. Deciding to act the part, he responded, impressing a tone similar to what he had heard in the detective films. "Well, schweet-heart, I didn't have the time to dress in the proper digs, if you know what I mean?" Ross instantly felt foolish. "I'm not sure how I got here, or really what the hell is going on. Do you know who runs this place?"

The cigarette girl brought her hand to her mouth and laughed boisterously.

"What's so damn funny? Would you keep it down?"

It didn't matter; the people in the hall didn't acknowledge.

She stopped laughing and shot Ross a cold look. "Okay, mister. If you're looking for the boss, turn around."

Ross turned and saw a well-dressed man wearing a brown pinstripe suit, along with a derby hat, shoes with spats, and a curled mustache.

The man approached Ross and proffered his hand. "Good evening, sir. I'm Roland Hiser, at your service."

Ross shook his hand.

"Quite a grip you have on you, good fellow."

Ross dropped his hand and looked back. He spotted the cigarette girl talking with other patrons.

"Quite the lively place we have here, don't you think, Mr. Delbert?"

"How the hell do you know my man?"

"A mere parlor trick, I assure you. We just simply read your mind."

"I'd say reading someone's mind is more than just a parlor tricky. It's pretty fucking impossible where I come from." He stood, reflecting on something Roland had said earlier. "You said *we*, Roland. Just who in the hell is *we* anyway?"

"Marvelous, Mr. Delbert, that's the right question. As I mentioned before, I'm Roland Hiser, and my partner … well, let's just call him Mr. Murphy. You'll meet him later; actually, he'll meet you, as you probably won't see him. Mr. Murphy will assess you. While we're on the subject of Mr. Murphy, I must say he is not exactly my partner per se but my employer. Mr. Murphy funds my work, but, in the end, he's the one who calls the shots." Roland removed a gold chain watch from his vest pocket, looked at it, and ushered Ross with haste toward a rounded booth next to the bar.

Ross quickened his pace.

"Time is getting away from us. Time is everything, and we mustn't waste a single second. Time bodes more worth than gold."

Ross was nearly flung into the booth. Just as he started to sit upright, Roland joined him. "Take it easy. You don't have to fling me around like a bitch. What are you doing? Falling in love?" Ross spat as Roland twirled his mustache.

"I can assure you I have no means of outward affection. We must dive into the brass tacks."

"Finally, what's going on?"

"I'll be blunt, Mr. Delbert. My partner, you, and I have a common enemy. I'm sure you already know his name."

"Nik fucking Vanelli."

"Well, I don't believe it is Nik *fucking* Vanelli, but it's Nik Vanelli just the same. You see, Nik is not only a threat to you, but to us as well. My sincere apologizes that we confirmed that with the methods we employed."

"What methods are you talking about?"

"It was a specter's doorway. Unfortunately, you had to witness the whole egregious affair, but it was the only way we could show you what you already suspected. I suppose after witnessing that, you want him dead."

"What the hell do you think, Roland? I don't know whether or not he knew she was married, but it doesn't matter. What I saw can't be unseen."

"Good, good, jolly good indeed. You can have your revenge and assist us with our cause," Roland said brightly.

"How can I do that?"

"Just think of yourself as a talent scout."

"A talent scout?"

"Yes, a talent scout. I want you to go to a bar called Hollow Grove tomorrow night. It's a little nothing place in the middle of nowhere located between Pemkey and Gibbswood. Despite its out-of-the-way location, it should be pretty busy for a Friday night. You should be able to blend in without notice."

"I don't know how to get there."

"Don't worry about finding it. After you return home, you'll find it just as easily as you can find your mouth with a fork and spoon."

"Why does it have to be there?"

"I'll be acquiring it soon. Think of it as an expansion project, a merger, if you will, between this place and a more ideal location. When I was there the other day, I met an interesting fellow I think would be a prime candidate to help with your problem—our problem. Mr. Murphy will help you identify him. Just think of Mr. Murphy as an angel on your shoulder. You'll know the subject instantly. I think you'll appreciate his reputation and moxie."

"What do I do once I see him?"

"You'll offer him money. You'll offer him every bit of the three thousand dollars you have hidden in the rafters in your garage."

"But that's my rainy-day stash! I won't offer him that!"

"You can, and you will. Mr. Murphy wants to critique this man, and you'll help me to deliver him. After all, I think we've given you something of worth. We've given you the identity of the man who caused your wife to act on her infidelity. That information has to be worth something in itself, doesn't it?"

"What if he doesn't accept the job?"

"Frankly, my good man, I don't give a shit. Mr. Murphy will judge him accordingly on whether he will be of service. If Mr. Murphy finds him unworthy, I can use him instead. Besides, you should be glad if he refuses. If he takes the money and the task, you'll be indebted to Mr. Murphy. Believe me, Mr. Delbert, it would be best for you if Mr. Murphy does not deem him ideal. Anyway, you owe me for the information. All you have to do is make an appearance and talk to the man. If you were a real man, you would take care of this personal issue yourself. I think the man you are about to meet just might agree."

"I'll do what you ask. Nik Vanelli will pay."

"Splendid. We appreciate your help. Use this information wisely. If the stranger helps you, it will cost you more than money—something in the lines of your soul."

"What soul?"

Roland's watch chimed, and the speakeasy faded.

Ross awoke drenched in sweat. It was Friday morning, and he had an important appointment. Ross knew where he needed to go.

CHAPTER 6
A FAVOR OWED

A strange feeling overcame Seamus as he pulled onto Observation Drive. He was actually pleased to be home. The streets were still, and the typical roaming thugs were not present. It was also satisfying to see Greg's minivan was nowhere in sight.

Seamus's tranquility was broken once he heard a voice call out, "Hi, Seamus!"

"Hi, Lynette."

"What are you doing?" Lynette walked toward the edge of her porch.

"I don't know yet."

"Do you have any plans for the weekend?"

"What about you, Lynette? Do you have plans? Are you going out?" Seamus nodded toward the entrance.

At first, Lynette didn't understand the gesture. After the thought settled, she knew what Seamus meant. Her dumbfounded look of infatuation disappeared.

Seamus walked onto her property, carefully placing his footsteps to avoid dog droppings. "Don't worry, Lynette, I promised I wouldn't say anything about you and Todd, but remember, you still owe me a favor." Something about holding the favor over her head exhilarated him. Seamus shifted from the blackmailing tone and returned to a pleasant state. "Todd can be nice when he wants something, but he can turn on you like a mad dog when he doesn't get it."

"He said if I can make him happy, he might consider dating. If that happens, I can move away from here and live with him."

Seamus shook his head with disgust. *You've got to be really desperate to want to live with Todd.* "Take care of yourself, Lynette," Seamus said before walking away.

"I will, and I won't forget the favor."

"Okay, Lynette." Seamus looked at her one last time before entering his house. *How could God put that ugly mug on such a hot piece of ass?*

Seamus closed the door, collapsed in his recliner, and retrieved his phone. *Should I try to get a hold of Elizabeth? God, I miss her, especially after looking at Lynette's fine ass.* Even though Seamus knew what would happen if he did, he put aside his better judgment and placed the call. With each ring, his heart sank. It went to voicemail. *Fucking predictable.* Seamus ended the call without leaving a message. Maybe if he sent a text, he would have a better chance for a response.

Seamus pulled the reclining lever, reached for the television remote, and selected channel eleven. The Comet Station was running a horror marathon. A couple of campy movies might hit the spot.

The first movie was a strange black and white flick with a blonde woman who Seamus regarded as attractive for the era. The movie started with no exposition. The blonde was riding with her friends in a drag race against a couple rowdy guys, she and her friends went over the side of a bridge, and she was the only survivor. Seamus was not surprised to discover she was actually a ghost.

The second movie was a little better. It was about two medical students studying death and the reanimation of corpses. The kind medical student reminded Seamus of the actor who played Lone Star in *Spaceballs*. The corrupt medical student reminded Seamus of the local pervert who used to live in Bradford, Herbert the Pervert. It was ironic that the corrupt character was also named Herbert. The flick was a bit deranged, but he enjoyed watching the kind medical student's naked girlfriend being held captive by the villain's headless body.

The last movie was the only title he remembered—*I, Madman*. It struck a sympathetic chord as he found the villain relatable. The villain went through murderous methods to please the object of his affections. *You'd have to be truly crazy or in love to cut off parts of your own face, kill people, and graph their parts to your face just to please a woman.* Seamus caressed his face as the credits rolled. *Maybe if I was better looking, Elizabeth would love me.* Seamus turned off the television and tossed the remote.

I can't sit here like a bump on a log. I deserve a good time just as much as the next person. His resolve carried him to his bedroom. He grabbed his leather jacket, black jeans, and his boots from the closet. *Hell, the last time I wore this, I met Elizabeth. Maybe wearing it again will bring me luck.* Before he changed clothes, he realized he smelled terrible.

He dashed to the bathroom and stepped into the shower. The water hit him with a surge. Once he finished and dressed, he decided he would go to Hollow Grove. It was the place he'd had his recent success. Seamus also wanted to find out more about what was transpiring between Mack and the stranger.

The evening air caressed his flesh as he stepped outside.

Lynette was sitting on her porch. Her eyes followed him.

What a crazy bitch. She lets Todd do whatever he wants, then she looks at me with fuck-me eyes. I bet she goes off like a rocket. I wonder what it would be like. Hell, you've probably never lived until you've had sex with a crazy person. It was an absurd yet enjoyable thought.

Seamus backed out, affording modest attention. *If there's anyone behind me, they'll move. Fuck 'em if they don't.* Seamus blazed through the subdivision.

Hollow Grove was busy. It was usually hopping on the weekends, but on this night, it was busier than usual. An orange full-size pickup truck sat in his usual spot, so he backed into the space next to it. The truck looked like it was a vehicle for hire. Delbert's Tree Removal Service was scrolled in black letters on the door. A strange feeling came; he could not discern whether it was destiny or some other force, but he knew he would become acquainted with the owner.

Seamus felt compelled to do his usually ritual, so he peered inside the gap in the fence. Nothing was present but overgrown grass. The autoclave object, its cover, and the supporting tubes were gone. Seamus withdrew his head and walked along the cobblestone wall. The sound of an electrical hum greeted his ears. After listening briefly, the sound transitioned into ethereal voices. Seamus tried to understand the voices, but they were unclear. After he rubbed his ears, the sound was gone. All that remained were the natural sounds of the evening.

The bar patrons were carrying on loudly, competing with the loud music. Along with their voices, "Tush" by ZZ Top blared through the walls.

Upon entering, Seamus noticed Mack seemed unnaturally jovial as he conversed with a customer. *Now I know shit is getting weird; Mack's never in this good of a mood.* After looking closer, Seamus saw something stranger than Mack's good mood.

A black-clad figure was leaning over the shoulder of a portly man. The figure seemed wrong. No one in the bar seemed to acknowledge him talking to the portly man. It wasn't just the lack of acknowledgment that made Seamus nervous but also his attire. The stranger wore clothes from different periods of time. His appearance was a blend between an undertaker from the old-west and a Nazi officer. The figure must have sensed Seamus, because he stopped whispering to the man and faced Seamus. He grinned and displayed large, foreboding teeth.

My god, did this weird fucker hear my thoughts?

With forced courage, Seamus made his way. The stranger and Seamus met in the center. He smiled at Seamus again. This time, Seamus got a better look at his face; it looked like wax.

"How are you doing on this most illustrious evening?" the stranger asked, extending his bony finger up the bridge of his nose, pushing up his pince-nez glasses.

"I'm good," Seamus responded, maintaining his guise of courage.

The stranger leaned forward and flared his nostrils. It felt like he was inhaling Seamus's soul. "I don't have any use for you, but that doesn't mean you don't have potential."

"Keep talking, fruitcake! I'll stomp your throat!"

"You've got moxie. Perhaps we'll meet again, and you'll be useful after all. Perhaps my assistant will find favor in you." The stranger wrung his hands.

"Maybe my pointed boot will find favor with kicking your horsey teeth down your throat," Seamus blatted as the figure floated away. "Goddamn weirdo," he murmured before sitting next to the portly man.

The portly man seemed unfazed by the earlier conversation.

Seamus studied him closer and discovered the same words scrolled on the truck outside were also on his orange shirt. Seamus tapped the bar counter to get Mack's attention.

"What do you want?"

"I'd like a shot of Jack Daniel's and a Busch Light. You should know that."

"Watch your tone, wiseass. I was having a good night until you showed up."

"You're always the warm and welcoming person, Mack."

"I don't want to hear it. I'm still not in the best of moods with you. I don't care that you brought the pain to Sweeney—I'm sure the cocksucker had it coming—but when he came stumbling back in, he looked like he had been hit by a car."

"He looked like he's been hit by a car?"

"That's what I said."

"Really?"

"Didn't you hear me?"

"I must've taken it easy on Sweeney. Usually when I'm done, he looks like he got hit by a train."

"I don't care whether you think you took it easy or not. It looked like a horror show."

Seamus downed the shot without effort and followed it with a gulp of beer.

"It sounds like you've got quite the reputation," the portly man said.

"You could say that. I don't start shit, but when push comes to shove, I don't have a problem finishing it."

"A big moxie fellow like yourself, I bet you could crack some heads if you needed to ... or wanted to."

Seamus set down his beer. His spine tingled from the man's words. *Moxie* was the same word that half-dead motherfucker had used. "Alright, you pudgy bastard. Where are you going with this? That strange motherfucker you were just talking to said *moxie*."

"What are you talking about? I was sitting by myself until you showed up. Are you fucking crazy? Regardless of what you think you seen is not important. I'd like to talk business. Besides, it's probably better if you are crazy."

"I don't know where you're going with this, but I don't think I want to hear it."

"Whoa, whoa, whoa, let's start over. I'm talking all this crazy shit, and you probably think I'm crazy. My name is Ross Delbert, and you are?" Ross proffered his hand, but Seamus did not return. "I'll get to the point. Do you know a guy named Nik Vanelli? I don't know him either, but I know he plays in a local band."

Seamus only afforded partial attention. The only aspect of Ross's question that stuck out was the name Nik. Seamus remembered Kenny's companions talking about him. "I don't know Nik Vanelli. Besides, if I did, what's it to you?"

Ross drew in a sharp breath and exhaled it like an angry bull. "That bastard fucked my wife, and I want his ass crippled!"

"How do you plan on crippling this guy? From the looks of you, I don't think you'll be crippling anyone soon."

"That's where you come in. I know his band is playing at Jeanelle's Bar in Gibbswood next weekend. Hell, my ex-wife's niece is dating one of the band members. My niece was the one who told me about their show. Despite me and her aunt splitting up, she and I are still pretty close."

"I don't care about you and your niece's relationship. What do you want?"

"Sorry, sometimes I tend to trail off. Anyway, I'd like to offer you a job. I'm going to make an appearance at their show with my wife. I want the bastard to see her and me together while he's on stage. I want to catch him off guard. That's where you come in. After I confront him, I want you to blindside him. I'll pay you three thousand dollars."

Seamus took another drink. "Let me get this straight. You want to pay me for tearing up some motherfucker I don't even know? Am I hearing you right? You want me to fuck him up and go to jail, while you deny everything?" Seamus's rage grew as his thoughts gravitated to Elizabeth and what he would do to her if she had done that to him. "What kind of man are you, Ross? A real man does the job himself. Bust his ass by any means necessary. Sucker punch him if you have to. If that doesn't work and he kicks the shit out of you, then kill his ass. Kill his ass and your cheating whore's." Seamus pounded on the bar to gain Mack's attention. "Give me another shot, Mack, and tally up my bill."

Mack poured Seamus's drink and collected his money.

Seamus tipped the glass and swallowed without effort. "If you want this motherfucker done, you better do it all the way. Show him that no one, and you mean no one, fucks your woman without paying hell," Seamus said before standing to leave the bar. Dark thoughts of Elizabeth cheating on him plagued his mind as he approached the entrance. The evening breeze cooled his body, but his anger lingered.

Seamus grinned wickedly, thinking about what he had said. *I'd do the same, but I'd make sure they suffered.* Dark fantasies played within his mind. Killing them would bring him joy. Realizing this disturbed him, and he wanted to free himself from the thought. He diverted his glance toward the lamppost and startled with terror.

The stranger who had been talking to Ross stood under the lamppost, waving.

Seamus looked away and walked toward his car. When Seamus looked back, the figure was gone. The insane Houdini act was the final straw; he'd seen enough freaky oddities to last him a lifetime. All he wanted was to go home.

"Garrett Ray, you cut that shit out right now! If you interrupt my show one more time, I'll take a switch to your ass!"

That was the first sound Seamus heard as he awoke. He glanced at his alarm clock—10:10 a.m. Regardless of sleeping in, he still felt exhausted. He rolled over and closed his eyes. As his field of vision turned gray, he entered the transition between sleep and consciousness. Loud cracking sounds ensued, and he was jostled.

"Godammit, Garrett Ray, now you're going to get it!" John Hermann shrieked.

Seamus sprung from his bed, walked to his window, and watched the drama unfold below.

One of the Hermann kids had fashioned a collection of faded red and blue gas cans into a homemade drumkit. The kid turned his attention from his house to his cans and burst with laughter while beating the cans with his plunger handle drumsticks. If the boy's goal was to infuriate his father, it was achieved.

John Hermann marched out of his house. John resembled a younger version of Greg Buckland. The only difference was John's hair was longer and darker. John was holding a bungee strap.

The boy's laughter stopped, and his smile faded as John advanced.

Only a second of silence occurred before John exploded. In a flash, John kicked the gas cans, and they toppled in multiple directions. One of the blue gas cans flew onto Seamus's property.

The Hermann kid, terrified, started to crab-crawled away.

Oh shit, this kid's going to get it now.

John grabbed the boy's arm and brought him to his feet. John reared back in a full swing and struck his son with the metal hook end of the strap. John gritted his teeth as each blow landed.

The rest of the Hermann brood spilled out and gathered behind their father. Some of the children were horrified, while the others were enthused. None of the children made a sound.

Whether it was by exhaustion or satisfaction, John finally stopped striking the boy. "Get your asses inside right now, or you can all line up for a turn! When I say shut the fuck up, I mean *shut the fuck up!*"

The children scurried toward the house, nearly running on top of each other.

John marched behind them, corralling them like sheep.

The punished boy remained on his knees, crying. Tears sizzled down his red-hot face. The boy scrambled to his feet. Red and brown spots appeared on the boy's posterior.

Seamus was sure the red marks were blood but wondered what the brown spots were. Seamus cringed. *If that's shit, that gives true meaning to the phrase whip the shit out of someone.* Seamus heard one of the boy's sibling's tease, "Garret Ray pooped his pants."

Seamus felt a moment of remorse but quickly purged the feeling; his attention rested on the gas can that had flown into his yard. Urgency beckoned Seamus to retrieve it. He did not know why he wanted it. *What the hell is so important about a gas can?* Nevertheless, he fetched an old, worn-out t-shirt and jean shorts from his drawer. Once dressed, he dashed to the utility room. He spied the cupboard above his washer and dryer. Seamus grabbed a pair of safety gloves from the bottom shelf.

He pinched the collar of the gloves and slid them on, along with a pair of worn sneakers, before stepping out. Seamus carefully guided his steps on the chipped concrete back porch slab. Once in the back yard, Seamus soccer dribbled it with quiet taps. After a tactful kick toward the back porch, he grabbed it and flung open his screen door and tossed it to the side of the dryer. Once inside his utility room, Seamus carefully removed his gloves and placed them in the cupboard. Now that he had it his possession, he could focus on other things. He turned his attention toward his back yard.

With everything that was happening in his life, he realized he had been neglecting his yard and housework. *I might live amongst trashy people, but that's no reason for my property and house to look like shit.* Seamus stepped out and pulled his lawnmower from his decrepit shed and filled it. The mower took some encouraging to start before it erupted with an obnoxious roar. Seamus began his day with outside chores. He saved cleaning his gutters last.

Just as he was about to climb down his ladder from cleaning his gutters, he heard voices coming from Buckland's porch. Greg was shouting at Lynette. "I'm heading out tonight! You better stay home! Travis is watching the house!"

"I won't go anywhere, Dad," she replied as their dog barked.

"It'd be in your best interest! Travis said he thought he seen you getting into a man's truck! He wasn't sure if it was you or not, but if I find out it was, there'll be hell to pay!" Greg shook his fist at Lynette.

Seamus turned away before they noticed him watching.

The Bucklands' dog turned his attention to Seamus and barked.

Greg commanded it to shut up as he pulled the dog inside.

Seamus turned and saw Lynette studying his body.

Greg yelled for her, and she dashed inside.

Seamus descended his ladder and placed it on the rack inside his shed, then went inside to clean his house. Where did this motivation come from? *First, there was the gas can. Why in the hell did I pick that up, and why am I doing all this cleaning? Does this mean I'm going to have someone over?* Seamus closed his eyes.

Were these thoughts premonitions? He hoped so as he located his phone in his bedroom and activated it, but his hopes were soon shattered. There were no missed calls or messages. Just before he shut it, he realized it was after three o'clock. *Where did the time go?* Seamus considered contacting Elizabeth to see if she was available but decided to wait until after he showered. There might be a better chance for a reply if he waited.

Once he finished with his shower, he selected a tight black t-shirt and dark blue jeans. Naturally, his black boots would be a part of his attire. If he was going to see Elizabeth, he wanted to dress to impress.

A text message would not suffice; he would call her to hear her voice. Something about hearing her voice made it sweeter. Seamus selected her number and pressed Send. After a single ring, it went to voicemail. Seamus fumed as the automated voice message patronized him. Despite his annoyance, he cleared his throat and spoke pleasantly. "Hey, babe, I just wanted to see what you're doing. I hope to hear from you."

"Goddammit! I worked hard all day on the house! Why the hell did I even bother?" he shouted as he paced the floor. After his irritation subsided, he felt a sense of revelation. "I'm not going to sit on my ass. This is my first weekend off from the new job; I'm going to have a good time."

If I go out tonight, which come hell or high water I will, I sure as hell am not going to Hollow Grove. Instead, he wanted to go to Maxwell's. The local venue seemed to be the best choice. Still feeling frustrated, he decided to smoke a cigarette and relax. As he stepped out of his house, he saw Lynette standing in the driveway.

"Hi, Seamus." Lynette looked around cautiously.

"Hi, Lynette."

"Dad's going out tonight, and he'll be out all night. You probably heard him say he's got eyes on me. I want to go out, but I don't want any trouble."

"Jesus, Lynette! You're a grown woman. You shouldn't have to worry about people tattling. I'll tell you what, I'm heading out later, and if I see anyone watching, I'll give you a signal. Just look for a weird gesture so you know to go home."

Her face brightened, and a large toothy smile appeared. She looked back as she stood on her porch. Her expression conveyed numerous emotions: *Why don't you ever take me out? I'd go with you in a heartbeat.*

Seamus smoked his cigarette to the filter and flicked it. Upon entering his house, his body felt heavy as he traipsed to his recliner. Sleep hit him like a ton of bricks.

The darkness of the evening came through his windows and snapped him into consciousness. He fluttered, wondering how long he had slept. Seamus resented that he'd slept the day away. It was 8:49 p.m., and he still had time to enjoy his night. Seamus spent little time before leaving.

A strong feeling inhabited Seamus. One way or another, his evening would be fruitful. Seamus scanned his neighborhood as he progressed down Observation Drive. None of his trashy neighbors were lurking around. The only person he saw was Lynette standing by the entrance.

As he started to pass by, she leaned forward and fixed her eyes.

Seamus only offered her a friendly wave. When Lynette was no longer in sight, he rolled his eyes. He traveled through Bradford until he arrived at the intersection of Railroad Street and Main before making a slow right toward downtown. After traveling a few blocks, he turned left into the closed Amoco gas station parking lot and backed his car next to the building.

Seamus stepped out and strutted across the quiet street toward the rundown bar. Upon entering, Seamus was greeted by a haze of cigarette smoke and the stench of stale alcohol. The drowning sound of country music offended his ears. Seamus kept his head low while passing a group of boisterous patrons; he did not want to pay their senseless banter any attention as he traversed the length of the bar. Fortunately, he found a seat at the far corner.

Stella Maxwell, the co-owner of the establishment, asked him what he wanted.

Seamus devilishly eyed the well-built cougar before requesting two shots of Jack Daniel's and a bottle of Busch Light.

Stella smiled at him while appreciating his wandering eyes.

Seamus downed the two shots but nursed the beer. After he emptied the bottle, he requested another from Stella.

She leaned over and handed it to him. Her sleazy cleavage greeted his eyes.

Nice tits for an older broad. I wonder how much those puppies cost.

Stella and Seamus engaged in conversation until their attention was diverted.

Todd Lawson staggered through the entrance while hollering over his shoulder. "Get your ass in here. We still have some partying to do before we get to the business." Todd pulled Lynette by the wrist.

Lynette reluctantly quickened her pace.

Todd and Lynette stumbled to the end of the bar.

Of all the places in here, they had to sit next to me.

Todd sat first while Lynette took the farthest seat. The smell of booze floated off Todd. "What's going on, Van Leer?"

"I'm just getting my drink on."

"That's pretty fucking obvious if you're in a bar."

Seamus turned his attention to the front.

Todd began to coerce Lynette. "C'mon, baby, you're supposed to be fun, not a fucking drag."

"I don't feel comfortable. I'm afraid I'll get in trouble."

"Trouble! Trouble! Trouble! That's all you think about. That's why we'll never be together. Jesus Christ, girl, you're a grown-ass woman. Act like it; get up on that pool table and shake your ass."

Lynette regarded Seamus with desperation.

Seamus only shrugged.

Todd stood and clumsily reached into his pocket while shambling to the jukebox. Todd made his selection and dragged Lynette to her feet. "Get on that table, girl! The song is about to start!" Todd hollered, gaining everyone's attention.

Lynette slid off her sandals and climbed on the pool table. She looked around petrified.

Todd staggered to his barstool and demanded a shot of tequila before swiveling to face Lynette.

Seamus continued to look forward.

Within seconds, the jukebox sprang into life, playing Buckcherry's "Crazy Bitch."

"Move it, bitch!" one patron hollered.

"Don't just stand there, dumbfuck!" another screamed.

"Move your ass!" Todd screamed.

Seamus reluctantly turned to watch Lynette dance.

Lynette gained grace until the song was almost finished. No longer wanting to be the center of attention, Lynette went to dismount.

Seamus watched as Todd grew infuriated, screaming as she slipped on her left sandal. "What the fuck are you doing? The song isn't over!"

"I can't do this!" Lynette raised her voice in defiance.

Todd swiftly grabbed her shoulders and shook her. He turned her back toward the pool table and bent her over.

"Knock it off, asshole, or I'll call the police!" Stella screamed.

Seamus dashed toward Todd and pulled him off her.

Once Todd was spun around, he was met with a sharp right knee to his gut. Todd heaved, then vomited painfully. The vomit landed in front of Seamus's boots. In a moment of lucidity, as Seamus's attention was drawn to the puddle, Todd ineptly took a swing and missed.

Seamus countered with a fierce right hook, connecting with Todd's jaw.

Todd staggered and slipped on his own vomit, striking the right side of his face against the pool table. Todd groaned as he lay covered in vomit.

Seamus jerked Lynette to his side.

The bar fell silent.

Seamus grabbed Lynette's wrist and pulled her through the bar as she continued to put on her other sandal. Seamus and Lynette burst out and crossed the vacant street. Upon arriving at his car, he opened the passenger door and ushered her in before running across the front. Seamus struggled to get his car started.

After a little protest, it roared into life, and Seamus dropped it into Drive.

During the drive home, Lynette kept her face buried into Seamus's shoulder, saturating it with hot tears.

Seamus coaxed her to calm down once they parked.

Lynette sat upright. She blinked heavy and panned the driveway. She was relieved to see Greg's minivan was not present.

"Are you all right, Lynette?"

"I'm just scared."

"You're safe now," Seamus whispered.

She embraced him, and her body relaxed. She reached for his right hand that rested on the gearshift and brought it to her mouth. She smothered it with heavy endearing kisses. When she arrived at the tip of his index finger, she placed it in her mouth and sucked.

Seamus grew erect as she swirled her tongue. He brought the back of his head to the headrest.

"I love you, Seamus."

"You've had quite a scare. Some heavy shit went down," Seamus said, bringing things into perspective.

Lynette looked at him infatuated. She leaned toward him and pushed her tongue into his mouth.

Despite her awkward motions and her bucked teeth, Seamus matched her rhythm.

She pawed at his chest, lightly scratching. Feeling her building arousal, she reached for his left hand and placed it in the crotch of her shorts.

Seamus followed with his right hand, placing it under her right buttocks.

Lynette moaned as he softly squeezed. She nestled his neck with kisses. As he continued to caress her sculpted body, Lynette worked her way to his earlobe. "I owe you a favor."

CHAPTER 7
SAVAGE GUILT

Seamus hastily bolted from his car. Before Lynette could react, he flung open the passenger door and scooped her out in an impressive display of strength. Seamus pressed her body against his car.

Her back ached while her lower half stirred. Lynette directed her mouth to his neck. Her large teeth scraped him, but that did not impede his efforts.

The small jolts of pain enticed him.

Lynette knew if she had done that to Todd, he would have followed with a hard hand. The make-out session could have lasted all night if it was up to her. She may not be the brightest bulb, but she knew a good thing when it was happening. She didn't want to ruin the moment by mentioning the pain in her back. *To hell with it, the stiffness in the morning would be welcomed.*

Seamus reached around her and caressed. His hands descended skillfully.

Lynette closed her eyes and drifted into dreams. She moistened and encouraged his desires. *Fuck me! It doesn't matter if it's in the car, my house, or your house. Fuck me against the car if you want.* She conveyed her desires with fervent thrust.

Seamus displayed his strength again when he wrapped her legs around his torso and lifted her.

Lynette bobbed with ecstasy. Her silent pleas to be taken grew desperate.

Seamus understood and pressed a passionate kiss.

Lynette gasp as Seamus spun her around and carried her across the driveway. She would have received him anywhere, but in her fantasies, it always took place in his house. Something always seemed more intimate about sharing his bed. With Todd, it always happened in his truck, excluding a few times in his bed, but those experiences were never pleasurable; they felt like rape. Lynette had envisioned sex with Seamus and the following events; it was intoxicating.

Lynette stifled a giggle as Seamus fumbled for his keys. Her heartbeat quickened when she heard the lock click. The front door opened, and the scent of his house greeted her.

Seamus urged her to stand, but she protested; Lynette wanted to remain in his arms. He pried her body from his as she stepped down.

Lynette noticed the place was a modest bachelor's home, but being with Seamus made it feel immaculate. Her excitement increased as she realized she would soon know how his bed felt under her skin. Silence cut through the air.

"This is my house," he said awkwardly.

Lynette's fantasies made waves, but she was taken aback by his obvious statement. She knew damn well where she was, and she didn't want to waste any time talking.

Seamus grew nervous.

Lynette panicked that she might lose him to a change of heart. She had waited a long time to be with him. Even though he had saved her, this was her time. If his urge faltered, she would remind him of the favor. Hell, she hoped he would take a couple favors. She prayed his words would not be a rejection.

"Do you want anything to eat or drink?"

"I just want you, Seamus." There was no escaping her desire.

Seamus battled with thoughts of unease. First, he considered Greg. Seamus was not afraid of him, but he was afraid of what he would do to Lynette. If Greg found out, he would punish her without restraint. Seamus also considered Lynette's state of mind. She was incredibly immature. His last thought lay on Elizabeth. Despite his suspicions, he loved her with all his heart. *I love Elizabeth, but I only see her when she wants something. Is that all I am to her, just someone of convenience? I really wonder what she's doing now. Fuck it!* "What happens now?"

"I want to return that favor … right now."

Seamus carried her to his bed with reignited desire.

Lynette reeled from the ecstasy as she tried for his belt.

Seamus eagerly removed her shorts after he sat her on the foot of his bed.

Lynette then hastily shed the rest of her clothes. She wanted to assist him with undressing, but he denied her efforts.

Seamus may have saved her from Todd, but this was his moment, and he wanted to drive her crazy with desire. Before Seamus joined her, he took a moment to drink in her body. Unwillingly, he compared her to Elizabeth. It pained him to admit it, but Lynette's body was superior.

Lynette's fantasies heightened as she saw his member before laying back and spreading her legs.

Seamus was equally mesmerized by her curves. He paused when he looked at her moist vagina. *It truly is the prettiest pussy I'd ever seen.* Seamus was ready to go, but his mind traveled elsewhere. "We can't do this. I don't have any condoms." Seamus told the truth about not having condoms, but his reserved rested more on guilt than on lack of protection. *I don't know if I can do this. I love Elizabeth! Although, how could anybody resist that body? What if she gets pregnant? What if she has some shitty disease?*

Lynette's desperation weighed on her. Her mind scrambled for something—anything—to not lose the moment. A thought came from nowhere. She didn't know where it had come from but was grateful that it had—a lie. It was perfect; she even surprised herself. *Oh, thank you so much, brain.* Lynette craned her arms around his neck. "You don't have anything to worry about. I can't get pregnant."

"Are you on birth control?"

"No, I was born with a condition." Lynette pulled on his body, hoping her explanation would be satisfactory.

"What's your condition?"

Dammit! She hoped another lie would come. She was close to getting what she wanted and begged for the right words. Luck was on her side. "I have Thomas Syndrome." The words had just spilled out. She darted for his neck and engulfed it with kisses. *What made me come up with Thomas Syndrome?* She searched her mind. It took little time for her to remember. It was a degrading and unpleasant memory.

On one of the few occasions Todd had fucked her in his house, she had been met with an unwanted surprise—one of his friends, Thomas. He was around the same age as Todd but more disgusting in demeanor and appearance. Todd had coaxed Lynette into his bedroom so she could pleasure both men. Todd had positioned her on all fours and took her mouth while Thomas took her from behind. She had protested as Thomas entered her bare. Thomas had jabbed his small, erect penis inside her. *"Shut up! I'm snipped and can't get anyone pregnant!"* Lynette had relented and allowed both to take her. The memory haunted her as she tried to concentrate on Seamus. For a moment, Lynette felt repulsed.

Seamus could not see her face but felt something was wrong. Was the moisture on his neck from her mouth or tears? He freed himself from her embrace. Her face was saturated. "Have you been crying?"

She shook her head. "No, I haven't."

Seamus closed his eyes and felt Lynette's hand move toward his erection and guided it toward her.

Lynette grinded on him.

Seamus delivered a deep plunge.

Lynette moaned with pain as he bottomed out. The pain was momentary as she throbbed with pleasure.

Lynette felt amazing in a way Elizabeth never compared. It felt like he was deflowering her. Lynette's enthusiasms matched his as he continued.

She appreciated Seamus's gentleness. Hidden pleasures populated her mind. She sank deep into the mattress and into her thoughts. Lynette saw herself leaving Greg's house and moving in with Seamus. The second vision revolved around her and Seamus moving from the subdivision into a modest love nest for two, perhaps somewhere around Milbridge. Seamus thrusted while her pleasure increased. Her dreams and fantasies took her to a glimpse of a hopeful future.

As she traveled deeper, she saw her and Seamus standing in a quaint chapel during the late spring. It was only the two of them, along with a reverend, as they exchanged their vows. Lynette cried out with orgasm as the image blazed.

Seamus grabbed her ankles and drove deeper as she clamped her teeth.

A final vision came before she climaxed again. In this flight of the imagination, she sat in the nursery of their country house, holding their child, while she rocked in a chair sitting next to the baby's crib. Seamus entered the room and affectionately rested his hand on her shoulder. Lynette placed the baby in the crib, and they strolled together to their bedroom.

Lynette entangled her body around Seamus and shrieked. She held him close while he remained inside.

However, Seamus did not climax ... yet. Seamus was still solid.

Lynette grew curious. Asking him might ruin the moment, so she concentrated on his face instead.

He bore a peculiar expression. It did not appear that he wanted to stop; in fact, he expressed a look of deeper arousal.

Her eyes lowered. She was astonished with the amount of fluid she had released. Her eyes flared as she wanted more.

However, Seamus wanted to try something new. He brought her legs upright and thrusted.

In little time, Lynette erupted again.

Seamus lowered her legs and grabbed her hips. He turned her over and positioned her belly down.

She felt his knees shuffle between her legs.

Seamus pulled her hips and raised her posterior. His chest glided along her back. His heavy breathing touched her earlobe.

She trembled, not knowing what he was planning.

"I gave you a favor by keeping your secret," he whispered with excitement.

"I know, Seamus." She felt his member grind between her cheeks.

"I also saved you from Todd," he said, increasing speed.

"I know you did." She was still oblivious to his intentions.
"I think I've earned a second favor."

At once, she knew what Seamus wanted. She shuffled her body down the mattress and grasped the top of the headboard with white knuckles. She maneuvered her pillow with her forehead toward her mouth and bit down. "Do what you want," she said through clenched teeth.

Lynette's face tightened as she squeezed her eyes shut. She readied herself for Seamus's entry. Through her pain, she could give him new pleasure. *I want you to treasure this. No matter how much this will hurt me. I love you, Seamus. Take it, baby. I'm all yours.*

Seamus inched deeper.

Lynette was grateful he was gentle and did not plunge all at once. She writhed as Seamus moaned. The sound of his pleasure was beautiful to her. She wriggled as the pain blended with pleasure. She wiggled and struggled a little to heighten his thrill. Unfortunately, thoughts of Todd returned. When she and Todd would have sex, he never wanted her to express pleasure. Her time of letting Todd have his way with her was over. She belonged to Seamus—heart, body, mind, and soul. Lynette smiled with resolve through clenched teeth.

Seamus's excitement crept through his member as his climax was imminent.

Lynette flexed as hard as she could. She wanted to cherish his release. Lynette intensified his excitement with a visual display. She stretched her arms and splayed her fingers. She hoped Seamus would see her doing this.

Seamus reared up and dove deep one last time before collapsing on top of her. They lay together, her belly on top of the mattress and his on top of her back. Together, they pant in synchronicity.

Lynette required loving contact. She extended her hand behind his neck and caressed him. "Was it good for you, baby?" she asked through long-winded breaths.

Seamus did not respond. He buried his face in her back.

Lynette cherished this connection, along with the feeling of his essence seeping out. Even though it was not the orifice she would have preferred, it still esteemed her to feel the product of his bliss. The moment could have lasted forever.

Lynette had experienced numerous sexual encounters before, some she had gained pleasure from, while others had been motivated by force, but nothing compared to this. Still, she wanted to know—no, *needed* to know—what this meant to him. She had given something of herself that no one had experienced from her before. Lynette planted her elbows into the mattress. "Tell me how you feel. I need to know!" Lynette shimmied and pushed out his half-erect penis.

He rose to accommodate her movement as she rolled over. "It was fantastic, Lynette. I've never experienced anything like that. I don't know how to put it to words." However, a series of thoughts gnawed on his mind—thoughts he did not want to face.

Fear and guilt lay heavy on him. The guilt came first. It was now undeniable that Lynette was in love with him. His fear rested on what he had done. The act felt wrong, almost to the point of feeling like a rape. The word *predator* floated around his mind. Seamus reminded himself that Lynette was willing and wanting. It wasn't rape, but he still couldn't shake the thought.

Seamus suppressed his feelings. Instead, his mind gravitated to wondering what time it was. The hour was late, and he was tired. A calming thought traveled through his mind just before he laid down his head. Seamus assumed Greg would likely return home after sunrise, and he shouldn't have to worry about any drama if he and Lynette slept for a while. Travis would likely be sleeping off his high as well, so he would not have to worry about him either.

Lynette yawned and pulled him toward her.

Seamus reluctantly kissed her. Something seemed void about the kiss; he was not feeling the same passion he had felt earlier. Seamus had only kissed her passionately earlier because of his arousal. This kiss had been guised with false enthusiasm. Now was not the time to rock the boat. They greatly needed sleep. Seamus quickly released himself from her arms, slid to the edge of the bed, and rooted through his pockets for his phone.

Lynette eyed him quizzically. "What are you doing?"

Seamus didn't respond. He shielded the glow of his phone with a free hand. There were no missed calls or messages. This was the only time he was pleased to see no messages. "I was just checking the time." However, that was not the truth. He didn't even acknowledge the time. "So, Greg will probably be home late?"

"Yep, Dad's at some girl's house. I heard him talk about her with Travis. I think she lives in Milbridge. It's embarrassing, because I think she's closer to our age than Dad's age. If Dad marries her, then my stepmom will be like a sister. Isn't that weird?"

Seamus jostled when Milbridge came from her mouth. Could it be Elizabeth she was talking about? No, it couldn't be, but Seamus still had to know. "Does your dad's girlfriend have a name?"

"Dad never said. All I know is she likes to do that drug Travis sells. I don't like Travis; he makes me feel uncomfortable when he looks at me, and he's mean to me too. He's always threatening me that he'll tell Dad I'm up to no good unless I show him something." Lynette viewed her exposed body before eyeing Seamus.

Hatred toward Travis festered within Seamus. The local punk was already someone Seamus never liked, but after what he had heard, his blood boiled. Seamus regarded her with compassion.

Lynette darted her eyes back and forth, raking her mind for something to say. "I think she works as a stripper."

"Are you talking about the girl your dad visits?"

"Yes, I think Dad met her after he scrapped some copper from an old house. Whenever Dad gets extra cash, he likes to go to the strip club. It always grosses me out, because he likes to discuss it the next day with Travis. I hate it when they talk. Travis always looks at me when Dad mentions it. I feel so dirty when he does. I know he'd never do anything with me because of his friendship with Dad, but I still think if he could, he would. I hate everything about it when he goes there. I don't think it's fair he does that, then gets mad at me if I want to go out." Lynette fumed over her unsatisfactory home life.

In all the years Seamus had known her, he had never seen her express anger.

Her expression shifted from disdain to enlightenment. A tactful smile grew on her face. She placed her palms behind her back and positioned her chest forward, knowing Seamus couldn't help but to look. A concept Lynette understood more than anything else in life was she had the ability to use her body to command attention.

Seamus fixated on her inviting chest.

"I wish someone would take me away and love me. I'd be loyal and give him all of my love, mind, body, and soul—that is, if someone would have me."

Seamus didn't respond; he only stared at her.

Lynette moved in for the kill. "If someone would have me, he could have me any way he wanted—any way he could dream."

It was a glorious sight, but Seamus didn't feel comfortable with the subject. Seamus let loose with an exaggerated yawn. It was contagious, as Lynette did the same.

"I don't know about all that, but one thing I do know is I'm tired, and I think you are too."

Lynette stretched her arms and nodded through another yawn.

Seamus took one last look at her breast before setting his alarm for 2 a.m. He curled up beside her. They closed their eyes in tranquility.

A gray void greeted Seamus. He was asleep but still aware of his surroundings.

A troubling voice shouted, "Predator! What kind of man fucks an imbecile? It takes a special type of loser to stoop that low. I know why you did. It's because no one else wants you. Even now, your precious Elizabeth is fucking her friends. Even if she isn't, do you think she'd stay with you if she knew what you've done?"

"I was lonely!" Seamus shouted and recoiled.

"Loneliness? Loneliness is no excuse. She may not be retarded, but she's still an idiot. Not only did you violate her, but you butt-fucked her. What if people found out? They'd label you as a rapist, and they'd be right. You're going to lose everything. Your life is over if this gets out; you're ruined! You might as well be dead, just like your parents. Predator! Loser! Predator! *Loosssseeerrrr!*"

His eyes shot open. He sat upright and flung his legs over the side of the bed. He stared at his hands resting on his lap. *How could I have done this? What kind of person am I?* Sweat beaded on his forehead and ran down his back as he heard the voice replay in his head. Seamus nervously closed and opened his fingers. *Who knows what Elizabeth is up to when I'm not around? Hell, she could be cheating on me. For all I know, she could be Greg's mystery girl. As far as Lynette goes, who hasn't fucked her? She's probably been with more dudes than I've been with chicks. Who cares that she's stupid? She's a grown woman, and I didn't do anything anyone else hasn't done or thought about doing.*

A shrilling sound broke the silence when his alarm sounded. The bed rattled as he jumped.

After scrambling clumsily, he turned it off. *I must get her out of here right now!* After a panicked glance around his room, he gathered his clothes and dressed. Seamus urged her awake, hoping she would wake easily.

Lynette groggily asked what time it was.

Seamus commanded that she get dressed.

Lynette asked if he was alright while pulling on her clothes.

Once dressed, Seamus led her to the front door.

Lynette planted her heels. "You're scaring me."

"I don't feel right. I think you should leave before anyone sees you."

"I don't care what people think. I love you."

Seamus couldn't think of anything else to do, so he pressed her back against the door and kissed her. "I'll talk to you later, but you have to go … now."

"Okay, Seamus. I'll see you later, babe." Lynette hurriedly left as Seamus closed the door.

His flesh crawled from her calling him *babe*. He rushed across his living room to the window.

Lynette raced up the steps and froze as she stood at the center. She smiled and waved at him. She blew him a kiss before scrambling inside.

Seamus was in this for the long haul; Lynette would not be shaken easily. As he turned from the window, he heard a noise from outside, accompanied by dim headlights.

Greg had just pulled in. Lynette had made it in the nick of time.

Seamus watched as Greg exited his van, looking heavily intoxicated.

A voice called out to Greg from across the street.

Seamus watched as Travis approached, but their conversation was hard to understand.

Travis didn't divulge that Lynette had been with Seamus. Maybe Travis wasn't really that good of a spy after all.

Seamus eavesdropped on their slurred conversation until Travis dispersed, and Greg clumsily stumbled up his steps. Seamus stepped backward from his window as Greg stopped in the center of his porch and eyed Seamus's house.

Greg glared before opening his front door and stumbling inside.

Seamus entered his bedroom and sat on the edge of his mattress. His eyes locked on his ceiling. Surely, he would fall asleep with ease, but guilt played in his mind. It began to pain him physically. This was a new sensation for Seamus. He labeled this feeling as savage guilt. Sleep eventually claimed him. However, it was not rewarding.

On Sunday morning, he awoke at 7:40 a.m. Seamus wanted to avoid everyone.

CHAPTER 8
SPIRITS IN THE NIGHT

The alarm sounded at 4:30 a.m. Seamus was pleased it was Monday morning and that the work week was about to start. He looked forward to escaping his neighborhood—mostly Lynette. If he wanted to have any peace, he needed to get away before she could approach him. Surely, she wouldn't be awake this early. Nevertheless, he didn't want to take the chance.

Employing tact, he located his clothes in the darkness, carefully placing his footsteps. He stood in his bathroom, pausing briefly to gaze at his reflection. Sickness clutched him as he looked at the cabinet mirror. He firmly planted his hands on the sink and lowered his head. Seamus's sickness was attributed to the remorse he felt over what had transpired with Lynette, but it did not end there; it extended through the course of his life. He fought the urge to vomit. In an effort to soothe his sickness, he splashed water on his face.

How can one person be such a fuck up? I know better, but I still do these things. How could I have done that with Lynette? How could I have played with her heart? If Greg finds out, he'll be pissed.

I'm not afraid of the bastard, but I'm afraid of what he would do to her. What if he took it too far and hospitalized her ... or worse? How could I have done this to Elizabeth?

"I wish I could go back and change everything—the fights, the court appearances, getting expelled from high school!" His throat tightened. "I wish I could prevent the deaths of Kenny's parents and mine!" Tears fell as he dipped his head. He raised his head and stared at his reflection.

His reflection faded. The only image that remained was the bathroom wall behind him. Frantically, Seamus grabbed the cabinet door and flung it open and slammed it shut after inspecting both sides. The cabinet glass rattled rigidly. Once it settled, Seamus's reflection returned, but it was transparent. The strange image crippled him with fear. If he had been drunk, it might have been amusing. Despite the absurdity, he couldn't help but to think his reflection resembled the characters of the a-ha music video, "Take On Me." His reflection mimicked his movements. The second he stopped panning, the image smiled. It was out of place. Seamus never smiled that gentle and serene in his life.

His reflection put its palm against the mirror, and Seamus did likewise. Once contact was established, the reflection reacted. The image shook and changed. Seamus withdrew his hand. Seamus looked around to find his own environment was motionless. The movement only happened on the opposite side.

His reflection sharpened, and small, shimmering golden spots no larger than needlepoints inhabited it. Seamus blinked in a flurry. After each blink, the golden spots grew to the size of dimes then moved. Seamus blinked as the intensity of the spots increased. Using his arms, Seamus shielded his face from the glowing, blinding, yellowish-white light that projected from the mirror. After the brightness calmed, Seamus felt a cool breeze.

A new world lay ahead. Images fell from the top of the mirror. At first, they were basic geometric shapes of gray in a navy-blue field. Once they settled on the other side, they gained definable colors and structures. People and places sprung into life. His past resided on the other side. Instead of reliving the events how they had happened, he did the opposite. He walked away from the fights that had landed him in juvenile court, as well as walking away from the fight in shop class. Instead of his parents dying, he saw them sitting safe and alive at the kitchen table, conversing with him, until he staggered away to sleep off his drunkenness. Seamus didn't see any images of Elizabeth. The yellowish-white glow returned and mesmerized him as new visions materialized.

The final image revealed a possible present timeline; at least, Seamus assumed it was the present. The exterior of a varnished wooden door with decorative glass lay in front. It opened slowly, and Seamus stepped in. The place behind the door looked like a family home. A few toys lay to the left of the foyer. This must be a family room or living room. It was the most resplendent house Seamus had seen. He didn't know anyone who lived in a home such as this. He noticed an immaculate staircase that stood to his right.

He surveyed the hallway toward the kitchen. It looked like a set used for a cooking show. Seamus felt the hardwood floor under his feet. While he peered down, he became aware that he was wearing a pair of brand-new work boots. His pants and shirt also appeared new. His shirt captivated him the most. It was not a style of shirt he would have normally sported. It looked like it was from a high-end store. Seamus heard small children dashing from the room on the left.

"Daddy's home!" the voices gleefully shouted.

He bent down in front of two children who appeared to be four or five. One was a boy with thick, dark hair. Seamus felt the boy bore a strong resemblance to him. The other child was a girl with golden curls. Seamus wondered who the girl resembled.

"Hi, honey. How was work?"

Seamus had never heard such a warm voice in his life. He wrapped an arm around each of his presumed children and squeezed them. "It was good, babe. I'm just glad to be home."

A voluptuous blonde woman with wavy hair came into view, wearing a tight, white tank top with an athletic print on the front, along with a pair of pink shorts.

Seamus sized her up and beheld her legs.

She looked at him curiously as he ogled her. "You look like you've never seen me."

"Nothing's wrong!"

The children eyed each other and giggled before running into the other room.

Seamus scrambled for a response. "You've never looked better in my eyes," he said, maintaining his poker face that he'd never seen her before.

"You say that all the time. You said that on our first date, our wedding day, and whenever you want something," she said, ensuring the children were out of sight before placing a playful hand on his crotch.

Seamus almost felt her hand in the real world.

She looked to her side before shooting him a seductive look. "If my mom-clothes turn you on so much, I'll let you take them off me slowly after we turn the twins down for the night." She stepped closer while closing her eyes.

Seamus closed his eyes to kiss her but was interrupted as a breeze blew through the mirror, and the yellowish-white light flashed again. His fantasy wife's lips grazed his, but the moment was lost.

Upon opening his eyes, his body felt it was broken from a well-rested sleep. His reflection returned, and the strange phenomenon was gone. His neck and shoulders ached briefly before he rolled away the stiffness.

Did I dream standing up? Once reality was restored, he reached for his brush and groomed his hair. Seamus left the bathroom and collected his phone from his nightstand. It was 5:45 a.m.

Where'd the time go? His nerves stood on end. Seamus dashed through his house and jumped off his porch after locking his door. Despite running late, he could not help but to look at Lynette's house. The place was dark, and she was not on the porch. His tension relaxed, but he still had the task of reporting to work on time. The last thing he needed was to get terminated. Seamus anxiously started his car and sped through the Wiley G. Estates.

Seamus arrived at 5:57 a.m. A close, unobstructed parking spot lay ahead. Seamus committed to a dead sprint upon stepping from his car.

Shawn watched as Seamus embarked on a desperate sprint and smirked as Seamus readied his security badge. Shawn flipped the electronic control to unlock the door as Seamus waved.

Seamus thought his lungs would explode when he stood in front of Tina.

At first, she glared at him but followed with a smile. "You made it in the nick of time."

"Sorry. I had a little trouble."

"I want my people here at least five minutes before the start of the shift."

"I understand."

"Start on the trash rounds. I have Ox doing a special project, and if he finishes, he'll join you," Tina said, inferring Seamus would be handling the task alone.

A part of him wanted to speak up and say it was bullshit that Ox could just sit on his fat ass all day, but he sustained. Seamus needed the job and didn't want to cause friction. *Christ, I wait for now to employ control? I wish I'd have done this earlier in life.*

"Get to work!" Tina barked.

"I'm on it, Tina." Seamus fought his urge to have one of his classic outbursts. Instead, he collected some new trash bags and left through the cafeteria toward the warehouse.

While heading toward the dock doors, he saw Ox sitting on the floor scrubber. Just as Seamus started his rounds, he saw another lift truck parked by Ox; Kenny Elnor was the operator. *This is all I need.* Seamus walked, hoping not to be noticed. With a clear target of escape, he double-timed it.

Whilst clearing the rear of Ox's scrubber, he heard the big galoot shout, "Hey, Seamus!"

Seamus stopped midstride.

Ox redirected his attention to Kenny while Seamus eavesdropped.

"Sorry I missed your show, Ken-Ken. I couldn't get my car started," Ox said while Kenny afforded modest attention.

"You didn't miss much. Hexed played first, and it was a shit show."

"That really sucks, Ken-Ken."

Seamus feared Kenny would recognize him. Seamus couldn't stand it anymore and decided it was time to face the music. Kenny would eventually discover who he was anyway.

"What do you want, Ox?" Seamus asked. "I've got things to do. I'm already in hot water."

Ox eyed Seamus as his disgusting mouth hung open. He placed his meaty hand over it in an *oooh, you're in trouble* manner. "That's what I wanted to talk to you about. Aunt Tina was mighty pissed. She said if you don't show up, she'll fire your ass. What did she say?"

"She reminded me of the attendance policy," Seamus said through his teeth.

"I would've fired your ass."

How am I able to control myself? If this was any other situation, this fat mongoloid would be bleeding out of his nose and ears. "Is that all you needed? I have to get back to work," Seamus snarled.

"Yeah, you can go."

"Fine!" Seamus made it a few steps before he heard Kenny's voice.

"What did you say that guy's name was?"

"He's nobody," Ox said smugly.

"What's his name?"

"Saymus," Ox said with heavy spray.

"Are you trying to say, *Seamus*?"

"Yeah, Ken-Ken. Seamus Van Leer."

"Did you say, *Van Leer*?"

"Yeah, that's right."

Seamus left as fast as he could. Once he gained sufficient distance, he went about his business but morbid curiosity gnawed at him. *Does Kenny know who I am now?* He struggled with the urge to look back as he carried the full trash bag to the hopper. After tossing it and pressing the compact button, he turned to where Ox and Kenny sat.

Ox drove toward the center of the warehouse, but Kenny remained. Stormy emotions flooded Kenny's face. His eyes beamed with hatred.

For the first time, Seamus felt afraid of another person. Seamus tried to disregard the look but could not help to stare back.

Kenny made the first move. He sped toward the staged freight in the dock area but kept his gaze on Seamus. Kenny grabbed his load and crossed the dock plate.

Seamus did not linger. *He wanted to kill me. He truly wanted to fucking kill me!*

The first two days of the week passed quickly with little event. Seamus did not see Lynette when he returned home from work on Monday, nor did he see her before or after work on Tuesday. Wednesday arrived with a beautiful morning. The sun blanketed the landscape, and, for the first time that week, Seamus felt at ease.

He arrived at the parking lot early—5:45 a.m. He parked in the rear of the lot in an empty space in front of the rusted chain-link fence. Seamus laughed at the condition of the fence, thinking it was a poor means of security. Maybe he should tell Shawn about it. It would be a good way to start a conversation. After all, he had a little time to kill.

Seamus waved at Shawn as he passed the window.

Shawn sat with his face in his hands, engrossed in deep thought.

Not much of a security guard if he's not paying attention to whose walking into this place. He looks like he's got the weight of the world on his shoulders. I can relate. Seamus politely knocked on the security window. Seamus's tap must have been harder than he had anticipated.

Shawn shot backward in his seat and studied Seamus with daggering eyes before jabbing the intercom button. "What do you want, Seamus?"

"I have a few minutes before I have to start. I wanted to pop in and say hello. I'm glad I did; from the looks of it, you could use someone to talk to."

"I'll buzz you in."

Seamus stepped to the side of the security door.

"Take a seat."

"What's up, Shawn? Are you feeling all right?"

"I'm fine."

"It doesn't look that way, bud. Quite, in fact, it looks like you've got some serious shit on your mind."

Shawn turned to Seamus. "You've got to be careful with what you're doing and what you're about to do."

Seamus raised an eyebrow. "Are you talking about Kenny? Trust me; I don't want any trouble. I feel guilty about what happened every day when I see him. I know I wasn't the one driving, it was actually my parents, but I've tried my best to avoid him. Ox was the one who told Kenny who I was. I guarantee you I'll keep my distance. He looked like he wanted to kill me."

"I'm glad you told me, but I'm not referring to that. I'm talking about something else." Shawn leaned closer.

"What else could there be?"

"You need to be careful with what you're doing and about to do."

"What do you mean?" *I need to be careful with what I'm doing and about to do.* "What the hell's going on?"

"I'm talking about the company you keep. If you're not careful, they'll drive you to seek the company of someone else. Their actions could drive you to the point of no return. This could make you an ideal candidate for someone whose company you don't want."

"I don't have any idea what you're talking about. I think you know more than you're letting on. Who are you?"

"I'm just a security guard."

"I've got to go. If you get the balls to tell me what's going on, we'll talk."

"You're right. I'm sorry. I wish I could say more, but I can't. All I can tell you is what I've already said. Be careful of what you are doing and what you're about to do."

"I can handle myself." Seamus slammed the door and stormed toward the entrance without looking back. *What a weird guy. I'm not talking to him anymore.*

He checked his phone—5:55 a.m. He was on time, and Tina should be pleased. The last thing he needed was any trouble. "Good morning, Tina."

"I'm glad you're on time. I suggest you get started."

"I'm on it."

"If there isn't anything you need, I think it would be best if you get going. I have nothing more to say."

Seamus was taken aback. She had not been in the most pleasant moods with him earlier that week, but that was a one-time deal. He had been on time. *What gives? What's her problem?* Seamus paused before leaving. "What's wrong Tina?"

"I think it would be best if you get started. Right now!"

No longer wishing to question the issue, he left without another word. Seamus started his rounds at the dock doors. After clearing dock door 103, he looked to his right and saw the back of Kenny's lift inside a trailer. Seamus quickly made his way to dump his trash before heading to the dock office.

The sound of harsh shouting bellowed through the dock office walls. "Dammit, Darcy! Can't you do your job? Do I have to find someone else?"

"I'm doing my best, Jim. I didn't mean to clear the load from the system with hold product on it."

"I'll fire you if you clear one more load with hold product. You're costing the company money. Get it right or pay the price!"

No motherfucker should ever talk to a woman that way. If I didn't need this job, I'd wrap that cocky prick's head around his ass. Seamus respected the woman on the other side's privacy and did not look at her as he made his way. No longer in earshot of her sobs, he walked to the opposite side toward the associate restrooms.

Ox's floor scrubber sat in front. Seamus watched as Ox walked toward it from the restroom. Seamus remembered his interaction earlier with Tina and decided to confront Ox about it. "What's going on, Ox?"

Ox did not respond as he heaved his large body up the side of the scrubber.

"Enough is enough! What the hell is going on?"

Ox faced Seamus angrily. "I don't keep the company of murderers. Your family killed Ken-Ken's parents. You'd be best not to talk to me unless it's work related!"

Seamus saw red and closed his fist.

Ox's eyes widened, fearing Seamus would explode. Ox defensively raised his hands.

Seamus stepped backward to allow Ox to drive away. As much as he wanted to cave in Ox's face, Seamus withdrew and kept to himself.

The end of the day came, and he reported to the custodial office.

Tina signed him out without uttering a word.

The day had grown cloudy and cool as he trekked home. It was a fitting scene. It complimented his mood. The clouds increased as he arrived at the Wiley G. Estates.

Yeah, that seems about right, he thought as the darkness loomed. Driving down Observation Drive seemed like a funeral procession. His body collapsed in the driver's seat when he pulled into the driveway. Seamus stepped out and walked in front of his car. When he cleared the front bumper, he heard Lynette's voice call out. Reluctantly, he stopped.

The sound of rapid footsteps followed.

His eyes remained forward.

"I really need to talk."

"Right now is not a good time. I've had a bad day, and I just want to go inside."

"This can't wait! I need you to hear what I have to say!"

Seamus turned slowly. "What is it?"

"I need to talk to you about the night we shared ourselves."

Of course, this would be the subject at hand—the exact subject Seamus wanted to avoid. "What's on your mind?"

"Are we together now?" Lynette looked around nervously.

Seamus watched her eyes dance. He could tell she wanted to say more. All he could do was look at her desperate eyes. If it had been any other day, he would have gazed at her body. If he would have been in a different frame of mind, he would have invited her inside. The day had been rotten. Sex was the furthest thought from his mind.

"Can't you see I love you? I had feelings for you before, but after we spent that night together, I've fallen in love with you."

"I can't get into this now. I have to go. I'll catch up with you later."

Lynette's eyes lowered.

"We'll talk later. I promise."

Lynette shook her head as her stare remained on the ground. She stayed motionless as he walked away.

When Seamus stepped onto his porch, he looked back before entering.

Lynette remained in the same spot.

He diverted his eyes as growing guilt resided. Seamus flopped on his recliner and rubbed his eyes; it was the only thing he could do. As his body relaxed, he heard his phone erupt to life.

"Hi, babe. What are you doing?" Elizabeth asked flirtatiously.

"I'm just relaxing. What's up?"

"I was wondering if you could take me to a couple places."

"Sure. I'll be there as soon as I grab a change of clothes."

"Thanks, babe. You're my hero."

Seamus changed his clothes and felt fueled with motivation. As he drove away, he could feel Lynette's eyes follow him until he disappeared from her sight.

Joy danced inside Seamus when he crossed the railroad tracks next to Elizabeth's place.

Elizabeth sat on the side steps. She must have been just as eager to see him as he was to see her.

This was the first time in a long time he had felt joy. Before he placed his car in Park, she opened the passenger door and put her hand on his as he reached for the gearshift.

"Let's get this running done so we can get back here." She ran her ring finger down the middle of her chest.

Seamus placed his car in Drive and accidentally tromped the gas.

Elizabeth laughed.

He smiled with embarrassment.

"Smooth, babe."

"Where do you want to go?

"I have two stops, and they're both in Port Lucas. The first is the Beverage Barn. I want a bottle of honey mead. It's the only place around that sells it. Then I have to go to my friend's house."

Seamus directed his car toward Port Lucas.

Elizabeth navigated the way to the Beverage Barn liquor store.

Once Seamus parked, they exited and headed toward the barn-shaped structure. They walked hand in hand to the entrance. This was the first time Elizabeth had demonstrated public affection. Seamus was riding on cloud nine as they strolled through the store.

She located the honey mead and pulled him toward the cashier.

Seamus was saddened when they exited; he wished it could have lasted longer.

As they approached his car, she pulled away her hand and hurriedly opened her door.

He afforded a moment of silence before entering.

Elizabeth's mood grew stormy as she told him the directions to her friend's house. She led him through an older neighborhood. The houses were in worse shape than the ones in the Wiley G. Estates.

Instinctively, he activated his power locks and white-knuckled the steering wheel.

Elizabeth rolled her eyes and pointed across his body toward her friend's house.

Seamus slammed the brakes and turned. As the car stopped, they rocked forward and backward.

Just as their backs touched the seats, Elizabeth unfastened her seatbelt and stepped out.

Seamus started to follow, but she quickly scolded him. "No!"

"Why?"

"My friend is uncomfortable around strangers. I won't be in there long. It won't take away from our time. I promise." Elizabeth closed the door and pranced toward the poorly lit side porch of the shabby house.

Seamus watched as the door swung open, and a hand motioned her inside. Seamus wondered who this friend was and what they were doing inside. He looked around, hoping for anything to give him a clue. Seamus watched in silence.

Time passed, and his anger grew as five minutes became ten minutes until an hour passed. His legs cramped, and his temper ebbed. Pins and needles stabbed his legs. *Fuck this shit! I need to stretch my legs, and after I do, I'm going to march up there and demand to know what's going on.*

Just as he slammed his car door, Elizabeth clumsily stumbled from the house, flushed and uncoordinated. The sound of laughter followed from inside. She eyed Seamus while shoving something into her purse. "What's the matter?"

"I've been waiting over an hour! I'm pissed off, and my legs hurt!"

"Would you keep it down? I haven't seen Angie in a long time. I guess we lost track of time. Sorry!" She gave him the directions toward her house in frustrated bursts.

Seamus concentrated solely on the road.

Elizabeth seemed antsy and sounded like she was trying to clear her nose.

Seamus looked out the corner of his eye and noticed her rubbing her gums with her fingers. *Was this some sort of nervous tick?* By the time they were halfway between Port Lucas and her home, Seamus asked, "What did your friend give you?"

"Girl stuff. Don't worry about it!"

Seamus knew he would not get an honest answer.

Her mood lightened as they turned onto Bradford Road, and she cuddled up to him. "I'm sorry it took so long, babe."

"It's okay. I'm not mad anymore."

"Really? I'm glad, because I was hoping to get some as soon as we get back." Elizabeth started to work on his neck.

His body sank into his seat.

As they crossed the railroad tracks, she grabbed his member and massaged it.

Seamus tilted back his head before looking both ways. Elizabeth pulled on him as they crossed the tracks, but Seamus's concentration was broken as he looked toward the dirt road. He thought he saw something he should not see, especially this close to Elizabeth's house. Seamus could have sworn he saw Greg Buckland's van in the distance. He wasn't quite sure, as the day had grown dark. He redirected his attention so he wouldn't miss the turn into the cul-de-sac. Seamus curved around and shifted his car into Park. The moment his vehicle settled, he had his hands and mouth all over Elizabeth's body, squeezing her breast with enthusiasm.

She tilted back her head as he lifted her shirt and sucked on her nipples. If she would have known he was this good with his mouth, she would have demanded he use it more often. As her excitement heightened, a loud vehicle traveling on the dirt road distracted her. She watched as the van turned onto Bradford

Road. *What the hell is he doing here?* In a desperate act, she used both hands to pry Seamus away.

Seamus reared back like an uncoordinated baby. Once upright, he saw the rear of the van as it sped north.

Elizabeth's breaths were short bursts.

He looked toward the road, then back to her.

Her face was planted with fear. She slowed her breathing before speaking. "I need a rain check. I'm not feeling well."

"You look like you've seen a ghost."

"I have to go!"

Seamus watched as she darted inside without turning back. He waited just in case she returned. Twenty minutes passed before he gave up and pulled away. A multitude of thoughts and emotions plagued him as he drove home. At first, he felt anxiety, but by the time he passed Eisenhower Cemetery, he felt red-hot anger. He knew what had upset her—*that goddamn purple van!*

Seamus connected the dots as he recalled the conversations between Greg and Travis about the two girls and the blonde guy. He also thought about the store at Port Lucas Mall. Everything came into full circle as he entered Bradford. Elizabeth was cheating on him with Chelsea and Josh, she worked as a stripper, and she was the one who Greg had been bragging about watching in the three-way. All Seamus had to do now was confirm Greg's van was gone.

Seamus sped like a madman once his wheels touched Observation Drive. His suspicions were confirmed when he pulled into the driveway; Greg's van was gone. Everything he feared was true. The urge to vomit plagued him as rage crawled over his body. After entering his house, he brooded and paced his living room while reflecting on his thoughts.

A dark solution came to him at 8:45 p.m. Elizabeth and her lovers had to die.

Two hooded apparitions entered a dark and timeless hall. The dark beings joined in the middle and raised their arms; their black robes fell to the ground and melted away. One specter was Mr. Murphy and the other, Roland Hiser. The hall took shape, revealing Roland's speakeasy.

"So, Master, what do you think?" Roland asked.

"Seamus is not viable to my cause. Light still resides in him. I need someone whose soul swims in absolute hatred," Mr. Murphy said through his long teeth.

"What about Ross, Milord? Can you use him?" Roland asked anxiously.

"Ross may serve to be a decent puppet, but he'll not serve my greater purpose. He is too old and stupid. I need someone younger."

"How will he serve you if he is not the one to carry out your final plan?"

"Ross will take care of my threat, but he'll not be my pupil. After he rids me of my threat, I'll have him commit another murder before taking his own life. He was not the only person working for me. I had another puppet before Ross. I enlisted Samantha to seduce my target, but her roll is over, and Ross will play clean-up. Besides, nothing's more amusing than a good old-fashioned murder suicide."

"So, can I have Seamus?" Roland asked eagerly.

"You humans—or should I say, in your case, you beings who used to be human—are so impatient. Take Seamus. Bring him to your cause. Show him the image of his loved one acting with infidelity. I suggest you start immediately. Make sure you furnish him with the tools he needs. Manipulate his desperation so he commits his life to you."

"Oh, glorious day, thank you, Master."

"Our enemies will perish soon. No longer will they stand in our way. I sense your pupil is about to fall asleep." Mr. Murphy erupted into laughter.

The two spirits in the night celebrated in the time-forgotten hall. Their victories were imminent. Sorrow would soon be in the works.

CHAPTER 9
TAKE ME AWAY

Nightmares plagued Seamus. In his dreams, Elizabeth danced at a strip club. Wolflike men threw their cash—nearly their whole paychecks—at her with ravenous lust. Elizabeth accommodated the beastly men with extra services in the club's private booths and in the seclusion of their cars after hours. Seamus was helpless to intervene. The last image Seamus witnessed was Elizabeth entering Greg's minivan. As the passenger door opened, Seamus tried to scream.

Returning to sleep was impossible; his body was conquered with hollow sickness. Seamus hoped a shower would cleanse his body and mind. While standing under the falling water, his nightmarish visions continued to play out. No longer able to tolerate it, he turned off the shower and dried. Seamus sauntered to his recliner to relax and get a grasp on his thoughts. While driving to work, a singular question echoed in his mind. *What should I do?*

Unable to concentrate directly on the road, Seamus had a few near misses. Despite being careless, he arrived safely at

5:50 a.m. Seamus passed Shawn without acknowledging him. Looming darkness lay ahead as he entered the facility.

Tina sat behind her desk, holding Seamus's timesheet like it was a vile object. She raised her rotund head as Seamus entered.

He cleared his throat to engage her politely, but Tina did not return the sentiment. "Good morning, Tina."

"You're already signed in. Get started!"

Seamus left abruptly into the warehouse where he instantly became a pariah. Most workers were focused on their tasks, but others glared at him. Seamus knew the source of the drama— Ox. Wisely, Seamus kept to himself the rest of the day until Tina signed him out without uttering a single word.

The disturbing images of his dreams replayed all the way home. Lynette was not present nor was Greg's minivan when he pulled up. Whether Greg was with Elizabeth or not, he did not know. Seamus entered his house, brooding. He almost forgot to eat until late in the evening. When he did, he only indulged himself with a small can of tomato soup. At 9:00 p.m., he urged himself to call Elizabeth.

Surprisingly, she answered.

"Hi. What's going on?" Seamus asked.

"I'm just hanging out," she responded over the sound of loud music.

"I just thought I'd see if you had any free time this weekend."

"I'm spending time with Chelsea this weekend." Elizabeth sounded preoccupied.

Seamus could have sworn he heard Josh make a snide comment, then Elizabeth hissed, *Shut up*. "I'm pretty busy; I've got to go."

"Sure," Seamus said and ended the call.

A shiver climbed Elizabeth's spine as she set down her phone while Chelsea, Josh, and Greg snorted crushed bean.

"Are you going to do that line, little gal?" Greg asked.

Elizabeth sat, fearful something dark was approaching. "Oh, yeah I must have gone away for a minute." Elizabeth forced a smile.

"Good. I can't wait to watch the show. Any chance I can do more than watch?" Greg asked.

Elizabeth put the rolled twenty-dollar bill to her nose. "You know the deal. You can watch, but there's no way you'll ever join!"

Chelsea and Josh reclined in their chairs, feeling high.

"Sorry, gramps. She said no," Chelsea responded cruelly.

"You're not going to touch my woman," Josh said defensively.

Greg pondered whether he should threaten them by no longer scoring bean. They would likely call his bluff. Losing Greg meant nothing. Besides, he knew if they went with someone else, he would lose the pleasure of watching. Greg excused himself and told them he was leaving. Before stepping out, he looked back with hurtful eyes.

Elizabeth watched through the kitchen window as his taillights faded. "I'm done with him. I'd rather pay for the bean than shake my ass for it."

"It's pretty creepy when I see his *O*-face," Chelsea added.

"I'm cool if you all want to mess around, but I couldn't stand another dude in the mix. Especially a gnarly old dude like that," Josh added.

"You don't have to worry. I just scored a good deal with my girl Angie. She and I go way back; we used to have a thing. Even though it ended, we remained friends. I told her about my problem with Creepy Greg. I've felt this way for a while. The last time he was here, I got this really scary vibe. I got this feeling that he wanted me all to himself. It freaked me out more than it does with Seamus. It's crazy how things work out, because just as I thought about it more, Angie called me and told me she has a hell of a hook up with her new boyfriend, Darius. The only catch was I would have to come and get it. I needed a ride, so I called Seamus, and I scored it easily. It's better this way. All Darius wants is money." Excitement gleamed from her eyes. "Not only did I score a bean, I scored something else." Elizabeth removed a plastic bag from her purse.

"Fucking dude has got the coke hook up!" Josh said excitedly.

"Hell yeah, he does!" Elizabeth said confidently.

Josh's eyes widened. "Break that shit out!"

"Not tonight. We're saving this for Saturday. Don't worry. I wouldn't dream of partying without you." Elizabeth glanced between the two as their eyes locked on the bag. Elizabeth tapped the table to break their fixation. "I didn't finish my story!" Elizabeth barked.

"Sorry," Josh said.

"Go ahead with your story," Chelsea added.

"I was feeling excited about the whole thing when I walked out of Angie's house. Of course, Seamus was naturally pissed, because I spent a long time in there, but I didn't want him going inside. I'm sure with how prejudice he is with bisexuals, he has the same opinion about black dudes with white girls. Anyway, after we came back here, we made up. Oh my god! The things he did with his mouth made me want to drag him upstairs. I closed my eyes as he rocked my world. When I opened my eyes, I saw Greg creeping by. He drove up from the side road then cut in front." Elizabeth pointed to accentuate her point. "I was freaked the fuck out. Seamus must've known something was up, because he saw the back of Greg's van. I think Seamus recognized the van, and more so who owned it. That's another reason I don't want to hang out with Greg anymore. If he and Seamus know each other, that's too much heat. I'm afraid of Seamus. I know we fuck sometimes, and I think the sorry sack loves me, but I'm terrified of him. Hell! The first night I met him, I watched him destroy another person. I wish I never got involved with him. I know someday he'll go crazy and come after me—or worse, all of us." She shuttered.

"We'll always have your back," Chelsea reassured.

"Yeah, I'll fuck him up if he ever tries anything," Josh said arrogantly.

Elizabeth knew better; Seamus would easily obliterate him. She smiled and continued to indulge in bean and conversation through the night.

Seamus craved sleep. Although a part of him feared it, since he knew what waited ahead. As his body sank into his mattress, the realm of dreams enveloped him. A doorway stood in front of him as he became an unwilling spectator.

Three bodies interlaced in front of him as he looked ahead. At first, he could only see below their waists. The first body belonged to a man, and the others belonged to women. The room gained clarity. It was Elizabeth's. Seamus's feet froze to the ground as the man climb onto Elizabeth while the other woman used her mouth on Elizabeth's breasts. Seamus tried to scream but fell flat. During his last effort to scream, Seamus felt a presence pass through from behind—Greg Buckland. Seamus watched as Greg stepped closer to the bed and pulled his pants to his knees, then tugged on his member. Greg's vulgar bliss fueled Seamus's rage.

Seamus's feet eventually released, and he lunged toward Greg with murderous intent. As he sailed through the air, he contemplated who he would kill first. Seamus passed through the specters and landed face first.

Seamus planked his body to stand. A strange new place surrounded him. Red and gold tiles adorned the floor. It looked like a dancefloor pavilion inside of an art deco building. The people around him looked the part as well. They reminded Seamus of a black and white show he had watched about gangsters. At any minute, he expected men with Tommy guns to storm through the front door. With his curiosity piqued, he wondered if he resembled the people as well, so he surveyed his body; he was clad in his normal attire. *I hope I can blend in.*

The people around him didn't acknowledge his presence. They were bound to the rules of their own world. Seamus became aware of this and maneuvered to a booth at the left side of the bar filled with various bottles of liquor. A mirror donning a design of a shooting star with a shark profile—the shark's fin was the top point, while its nose and mouth comprised the right point and bottom points—hung behind the shelf of bottles. His eyes were drawn toward a man sitting in a booth—the same man from Hollow Grove.

"Seamus, my good man, how are you?"

"I've seen you before. You were at the Grove with Mack," Seamus said.

"Quite right. I've called you here because you need my help. Do you want it?"

"Yes," Seamus said instantly.

"Jolly good. All you have to do is wake up. You'll know what to do when the time comes."

The world around him faded, and Seamus awoke in his bed at 4:15 a.m. Surprisingly, he felt good. The time flew as he got ready and left for work. His spirits were high despite Tina's cold greeting. The only incident that transpired that day was his termination.

Tina informed him that his presence was troubling for other associates, and it was best if he no longer stayed with the company.

Seamus did not protest as he placed his badge on her desk. Seamus was now free to discuss business with the stranger.

While sitting quietly at home, Seamus eagerly waited for another communication.

No visions or dreams greeted Seamus as he laid down his head. All Seamus heard was the man's voice from beyond a distant void instruct Seamus to wake up and collect the materials set aside for him and wait for night. After Seamus acknowledged, he awoke to the midmorning light.

Seamus stood and stretched. Just as he was about to head to his bathroom, he almost tripped over a cluster of objects—the gas can he had stolen from Hermann's, a black plastic disposable lighter, and the clothes he had worn the night he had met Elizabeth folded neatly. On top of his clothes sat a note: *Here are the materials you need. Inside the gas can is an accelerant I developed to aid you with your endeavor. Use the veil of the night!!*

Daylight faded as the evening approached. Seamus changed into the clothes placed before him and stowed the lighter in his jean pocket. The gas can was the last item he gathered. He unscrewed the cap and smelled the vapors. Seamus could not identify the odor and feared the substance was unstable. He carefully tightened the cap and walked with care as the fluid purged.

It was ten minutes passed ten o'clock, and blackness gripped the sky. Seamus was not alone as he stepped onto his porch.

Greg watched from his own porch, smiling snidely.

Seamus was unaware of Greg's presence as he placed the items in his car. He straightened his posture and felt a tap on his shoulder.

"Where do you think you're going, asshole? Are you going to Elizabeth's?"

"I have business that doesn't concern you. Or maybe it does," Seamus said hatefully.

"Can't you see she don't want you? You don't have what she needs."

"Maybe you're right. I don't have what Elizabeth needs, but I know someone who does—your daughter. She wanted everything I gave her. She came like a motherfucker. Hell! She even came when I shoved it in her ass."

Greg stepped backward while screaming toward his house for Lynette.

Lynette dashed out and stood by her father.

Greg asked if it was true, and she bursts into tears.

She told a different story, accusing Seamus of violating her.

Greg bolted toward Seamus and pressed his fist against Seamus's chest.

Seamus bested him with a solid punch to his sternum.

Greg fell and doubled over.

Seamus delivered an onslaught of brutal kicks. The second-to-last kick landed on Greg's ribs. He heard a satisfying crunch. His final kick landed between Greg's upper lip and nose. Whether he'd knocked Greg unconscious, he didn't know.

Lynette knelt beside Greg, sobbing and babbling.

Seamus kicked a heap of gravel at her.

Lynette wiped the dirt from her eyes as Seamus pulled away, cackling like a crazed man.

Upon entering the rural area outside of Bradford, his mind shifted to memories of driving to Elizabeth's house. He recalled each journey and how he had felt yearning. What he craved now was death. The images of Elizabeth's, Josh's, and Chelsea's writhing bodies struggling for freedom from the fire excited him. Dwelling in his macabre fantasies was unwise; he needed to employ caution and attention to the road ahead. Fantasy would be reality soon enough.

Hollow Grove came into view. It looked moderately occupied as he passed. Something seemed peculiar about the place; it marked the point of no return.

His car crept like a snake in the grass as he slowed it while making the final approach toward the railroad tracks. Once his car cleared the first rail, he killed his headlights. Seamus stopped just as the rear cleared the dirt road. Stealthy, he backed slowly onto the dirt road.

Once mentally prepared, he readied the gas can and lighter before stepping onto the crisp, dirt road. Seamus employed the soft light emitting from Elizabeth's kitchen window to guide his way while he kept close to the ground, lingering in the shadows. Seamus knew this would be the last time he would see the place. His glance shifted toward the center of cul-de-sac to the island of trees. His gaze followed the curve of the cul-de-sac before it fell on Josh's car. He darted from one cluster of shadows to the other. The sound of music boomed from inside. Once safely secluded, he put down the gas can and retrieved a cinder block. Effortlessly, he heaved it toward Josh's windshield.

The windshield spiderwebbed while the car alarmed blared. The shrieking sound of the alarm overpowered the music coming from inside. Josh would surely come scrambling out to investigate. Once Josh would be in sight, Seamus would take care of him … permanently.

Seamus eagerly watched as Josh scurried past the kitchen window before running outside. *It's time to get on the clock.* Adrenaline coursed through Seamus's body.

Josh stepped out the side entrance, wearing only a pair of black leather pants. He scrambled barefoot to the driver side. "What the fuck happ—"

Seamus blindsided Josh with a devastating blow to his head. Seamus struck him again in the center of his face.

Blood and teeth went flying. The pain and shock rendered Josh silent as Seamus threw him toward the black shadows. He landed on his right side with an unforgiving thud.

Seamus mercilessly pummeled his head and body as Josh desperately clawed the dark ground, attempting to escape.

With his strength nearly depleted, he rolled onto his back and wondered who or what was doing this. He watched in terror as he identified his attacker.

Seamus flashed a murderous grin as he hammered his boot on Josh's throat.

Thick blood erupted from Josh's mouth.

"This'll teach you to fuck another man's woman," Seamus hissed. The sound of Josh's painful breathes were like a choir of angels to Seamus. Now it was time to punish the whores. After he was done with Elizabeth and Chelsea, he wanted to devote more time to Josh. It was only fair. Josh had the luck of escaping fire.

Seamus removed the cap from the gas can and moved swiftly. *This stuff smells awful. What is this shit?* Seamus thought as the odor overwhelmed him. He touched the flame of his lighter to the accelerant. The house caught instantly. Seamus turned to run away but was slowed when a hand grabbed his ankle.

Josh laid, pleading. "Help me! I'm sorry for what I've done."

Seamus jerked free and spoke the last words Josh would ever hear. "You're going to die—all of you."

Josh clawed for the ground once again.

Seamus slammed his boot on Josh's wrist. "None of you pieces of shit will have an open casket."

Seamus escaped toward the tree line of the dirt road. He swung open the passenger door and tossed the gas can inside his car before diving inside to flee. He sped away on Bradford Road.

Worry was the furthest from his mind; he only felt euphoria. The bitch and her lovers were dead. As he traveled, the thrill diminished. New thoughts dwelled in his mind as he approached Eisenhower Cemetery. He felt the cemetery was glaring at him with unremitting judgment. Elizabeth, Chelsea, and Josh would be there soon. Maybe if they weren't buried at the Eisenhower, they would be somewhere else. "What have I done?" he screamed regretfully. "I hated the others, but I loved Elizabeth. They'll fry me for sure!"

After frantically looking around, he realized he was approaching Hollow Grove. Seamus yanked the wheel and cut across the lot. Once stopped, he killed the engine and ripped the key from the ignition. The parking lot was moderately populated. Seamus hoped the occupants would remember seeing him and be too drunk to discern when they had. He needed an alibi. Seamus did his best to gain composure. After pulling in a deep breath, he opened the door, and a strange, whitish light shone. Seamus crossed his arms in front of his face.

His mouth fell open when he realized it was the same speakeasy from his dreams. Just as he made his assessment, the entrance slammed shut, and he saw the door had been replaced with a different one. Not wanting to regard it any further, he moved forward.

The bartender motioned for him to sit.

Seamus reluctantly complied and flopped on the barstool. He requested a shot of Jack Daniel's.

The bartender poured it gingerly.

What the hell's going on? What happened to Hollow Grove? Seamus watched as the bartender returned the bottle. The same *shooting shark* symbol rested on the mirrored liquor shelf. "What's going on here, man? What happened to Hollow Grove?"

"First of all, sir, my name isn't *man*; it's Niles. This is The Shooting Shark. I don't know anything about this Hollow Grove you speak of." Niles eyed Seamus in disbelief.

This had to be a dream. Everything that had happened and was happening was a nightmare. A firm hand grabbed his shoulder, and he startled before slowly turning.

"I can assure you this is not a dream."

"I know you!" Seamus exclaimed.

"Of course, you do. I'm the owner of this establishment. You were here the day Mack signed the place over."

"This doesn't make sense. There's no way you could've remodeled so fast. Also, the Grove looked normal earlier tonight. How the hell could you have done all of this? How could you have spoken to me in my dreams?"

The man looked around while other patrons greeted him. "Would you keep your voice down? There's no reason for you to act irrational. My name is Roland Hiser, just in case you don't remember. You're Seamus Van Leer. Before you ask me how I know, don't worry about it; that's not important. What is important is what we do about your situation." Roland smiled. "I know about the murders."

Seamus tried to flee, but Roland pulled him down.

"Please calm yourself. I won't report you, and no one here will do any such thing. No one will come looking for you here. I think it would be best if we spoke in private." Roland gestured Seamus to follow and led him toward the stage.

They arrived at a door with the word **Private** scrolled in an old-fashion font at eye level. Roland pushed it open and stepped through.

Seamus followed willingly and saw a narrow staircase leading to the left. Amazing sights greeted him upon arriving at the top of the blind staircase. The upstairs appeared to be from an entirely different time—a different world. In front of Seamus sat a futuristic lab with machines resembling something from a sci-fi movie, like a place beyond his proverbial grandchildren's time. After he gazed awestruck, he noticed a clear, hexagonal prism with mechanical components on top residing in the middle. It stood a foot taller than Seamus and a foot wider.

"It's a beauty, isn't it? It's actually my partner's design. It's not the original model; it's the finished product. The prototype is how I got here. I dismantled it and used the parts to create this."

"Do you mean that crazy-looking thing out back was the prototype?"

"Oh, so you've seen it?"

"I saw it through the gap in the fence on the day I met you. I also saw a bunch of weird lights coming from that window." Seamus pointed toward the only normal aspect of the room.

"Let me guess. You probably saw a specific pattern. White, green, purple, and blue."

"Yes!"

"That light is the heart and soul of this contraption." Roland approached the prism and entered a series of commands on a keypad on the front side. A canister dropped from the center of the mechanical housing, and a triangular orb inside no larger than a golf ball resided and emitted the same pattern. "It's one of the mystical orbs. There are three in total. This one is the orb of time and space, the other is magic and fantasy." Roland paused while admiring his orb.

"What's the third?"

"The third? I actually don't know. All I know is if someone holds this one, along with magic and fantasy, the third will reveal its identity. Actually, I'm still searching for the orb of magic and fantasy. I need your help. In return, I can give you great things."

"What sort of great things?" Seamus asked with disbelief.

"Well, I'm aiding and abetting a murderer …"

Seamus swallowed hard. "I'll give you that, but what else can you do?"

"As I said before, this is the orb of time and space. You could go back in time and fix your broken life—a total redo if you want. You could get out of this hot water you're in now. Instead of living as a loser—well, something far worse now, a murderer—you could live as a winner. You'll still be aware of the events from this life; you'll never lose those memories, but you could fix your past and, dare I say, even learn from them. The only thing I ask is for a single favor. I think that's one hell of a bargain."

"I can fix *everything*?"

"Yes, all for just a single favor. I'll contact you after you are established in your new life. Once the favor is complete, you'll be free of me and our business … forever." Roland offered a *trust me* smile.

Seamus looked from Roland then toward the machine. "When do we start?"

"It has already begun." Roland extended his hand, motioning Seamus to stand in front of the prism. He entered more commands on the keypad.

The canister released the shimmering orb and floated freely. The prism expelled a puff of white, green, purple, and blue vapor.

Seamus stared and concentrated on his hopes and dreams. A silent prayer looped as the orb produced an ethereal hum. *Take me away!*

Chapter 10
A Life Gone By

"The process is about to start. Are you ready?"

Seamus nodded.

"Listen carefully! The orb is going to read you! This is a rather unpleasant experience; to be truthful, it hurts like hell! Whatever you do, don't break contact! If you do, you could be disintegrated, suffer cerebral destruction, or become disfigured! Fight the pain! You're about to become part of the orb, and it will become part of you! We go in three ... two ... *one*!" Roland pressed the command key and retreated to the other side.

Seamus watched as the orb expanded to the size of a basketball. Its brightness increased while its ethereal hum blasted. Light engulfed Seamus—white, green, purple, and blue. Immense pain followed, starting in his feet, hands, chest, and head. It was a burning, freezing, crushing, and impacting feeling before new types followed. Seamus could not escape the agony. If he could scream, it might ease some of his suffering. Seamus gained new strength as the pain dominated him.

It was what he owed for the lives he had savagely ended. Eventually, he mustered a scream before it was sucked back into his mouth. A cyclone populated in the center of his chest and pulled his body. Fear gripped him as he lost his physical form. The orb's colors transitioned into whitish gold.

The light of the orb was no longer seen through his physical eyes, as his ocular fluids melted away. The orb pulled the cyclone that had once been Seamus Van Leer toward its center.

Seamus tried to pull in a deep breath but was unable. The human condition no longer applied. His cyclone increased speed as images of past events surrounded him. Seamus had a first-person view of the night he had rescued Elizabeth. He stood outside Hollow Grove and watched as Sweeney harassed her. Naturally, he wanted to intervene. As he was about to take the first step, his cyclone reacted. It pained him the same way it had during his metamorphosis. Seamus heeded his past body to walk away. A wonderful feeling of reward followed. Another flash of whitish-gold light shined. His cyclone spun as he vacated his past body.

The light disappeared as he traveled. Seamus found himself in his old home, sitting with his parents. His past body felt uncoordinated, but his cyclone was lucid. It was the moment before he had suggested more beer. Despite being drunk, he knew what he had to do; time was short.

Seamus acted desperately, springing from his chair and racing toward the bathroom. Once inside, he forced his fingers down his throat. Feeling burdened, Seamus hoped his parents would hear him. Time was growing short to actually produce vomit. While in mid gag, he cut lose as his parents entered. "I'm not feeling so hot."

"It looks like you barfed out more than just beer," Randy said.

Ida elbowed him. "We should call it a night. We'll be in the living room when you get yourself together."

Randy and Ida stepped away while Seamus lay on his back and looked at the ceiling. As the room spun, he couldn't discern if the feeling was from being drunk or if his cyclone was reacting. The whitish-gold light returned. His cyclone form felt triumphant as it gained motion.

Penguard came into view of his new eyes. Seamus stood inside the autobody shop class. Instinctively, Seamus turned toward Chris Rayle Junior and his buddies as they were about to rough up the weak kid. The vision was clear in both his old and new eyes as he watched the weak kid watch terror. Pain revisited Seamus as he approached the group. Seamus clutched his hand on his chest, hoping to suppress it. *I'll do it better this time ... I'll do it right.* The pain subsided.

Seamus stormed toward the boys as they had the small kid bent over backward on a four-station workbench. He gained a better view of what they were doing.

They had the boy's right arm stretched to the corner. Chris Rayle and his friends were trying to place the kid's hand inside a corner-mounted clamp.

Seamus threw off the boys and faced Chris.

The small boy hugged the ground.

Seamus stood ready for Chris's blindsiding punch; he stepped backward as Chris flung wide. Seamus intercepted and wrenched Chris's arm. Once in control, Seamus slammed Chris face.

Chris struggled as Seamus maintained his hold.

The other boys advanced, but Seamus ordered them back. They complied as they watched Chris writhe.

Seamus fought to remember his instructor's name while driving Chris's wrist higher until—*eureka!* The teacher's name was Fetzel. "Find Mr. Fetzel! I can't do this all day!" Seamus demanded, and the kid scurried toward Mr. Fetzel's corner office.

"What's going on here?" Mr. Fetzel shouted.

"Seamus went fucking nuts," one of the boys said.

Seamus soon remembered Chris's buddies name— Diamond Clayton.

"Watch your mouth, Clayton! Let him go, Van Leer! Somebody better tell me what's going on!"

"Seamus was protecting me," the weak boy said and stepped forward.

"Is that true, Van Leer? Were you protecting Ricky?" Mr. Fetzel asked sharply.

"Yes."

"Ricky, Seamus, wait for me in the hallway. The rest of you are coming with me. I hope you don't have plans this weekend. Your Saturday belongs to me." Mr. Fetzel ushered the boys to his office.

"Thanks, man, for watching over me. I know we haven't spoken much—at all, really—but I'm Ricky Kerr." Ricky proffered his hand.

Seamus accepted the shake. "I'm Seamus, and don't think anything of it."

As Seamus lowered his hand, light enveloped him. He felt different as he traveled back in time. The motion was faster, and light flowed through him. He readied himself as he was about to take the next leap.

Mrs. Maidmill's kindergarten classroom surrounded him. The unpleasant teacher sat on stool in front of the room, reading *The Three Billy Goat's Gruff* aloud.

Even though he had no memories of this event, a strong feeling followed. Seamus directed his gaze from Mrs. Maidmill to the boy sitting to his right—Davy Mueller. Seamus also noticed Lynette sitting at the table.

Davy grinned devilishly before blowing into his hands.

Mrs. Maidmill marched toward Seamus and Davy.

Lynette sunk under the table, terrified.

Mrs. Maidmill scolded Davy and Seamus before excusing the other children for recess. Davy tried to make for the door, but Mrs. Maidmill grabbed him. "Which one of you interrupted story time?"

Seamus remained silent while Davy looked defiantly.

"If you want to play it that way, none of you get to go to recess. You can just sit here with your heads down."

Seamus complied with the large, middle-aged woman.

Davy stood and flung his chair backward. "It was Seamus!" Davy shouted as the last of the children, including Lynette, headed for the playground.

"Okay, buster! Now you're in real trouble! I'm calling your parents!" Mrs. Maidmill shrieked; her long denim dress flew as she tromped.

Seamus rested his head inside his arms. Fearful tears rolled from his eyes. A whimper escaped his mouth before his cyclone reacted. *This was the day Davy trashed the room. We both got in trouble. The little bastard moved away two weeks later. Mrs. Maidmill took us into the coat closet and beat the shit out of us. Trouble followed me ever since.* Seamus's head shot up to find Davy. He remembered Davy had pulled Mrs. Maidmill's chair from behind her desk, boosted himself up, and kicked her papers to the floor before trashing the classroom. *I only have one chance to stop this.* Seamus ran to Mrs. Maidmill's desk before Davy started.

Seamus grabbed Davy's leg.

Davy lost his balance and fell on the black-and-white-checkered floor. Davy whimpered while Seamus frantically straightened the papers. Davy rose to his feet and tore ground to the far end of the room where Mrs. Maidmill kept the inflatable Letter People dolls.

Seamus gave chase and grabbed Davy's rat tail.

Davy yelped as Seamus gained control.

"Listen, you little fuck," Seamus said through clenched teeth, which felt strange, as his mouth still had baby teeth. Regardless, Seamus's resolve was strong. He had to act decisively, as he had with Chris Rayle earlier—which was strange to think about a future event in past tense. Seamus wrenched Davy's arm. "I'll kill you if you don't stop!" Seamus's voice sounded like an adult's. "Say that you understand and the hurting stops!"

"I'll be good!"

"Sit the fuck down!"

The clomping sound of Mrs. Maidmill's footsteps followed.

Seamus raced passed Davy.

Davy sobbed as he caught up to Seamus.

The sound of Davy crying was the first thing Mrs. Maidmill heard. "Why are you crying? If you can't take the heat, you better stay out of the kitchen."

Something clicked in Seamus's mind. Another memory flooded back. Mrs. Maidmill had always said that cruel catchphrase when a child got hurt or was in trouble. While attending his parent/student kindergarten orientation the night before his first day of school, everyone had remarked how she said that in her no-nonsense tone. The parents also stated they hated having another child pass through her class. *Thank God she's a kindergarten teacher. At least the kids will have her done and over with early.*

"Stop crying right now! It won't do you any good, buster. I've called your parents. They sound a might mad." She always said *Buster* and *a might mad* too.

Davy tried to force words. "I didn't do anything!"

"You did plenty, and now you'll pay," she retorted with pleasure.

"I swear it, Mrs. Maidmill!"

"I don't want to hear it!"

"I'm telling you the truth! He-He-He tried to hur-hur-hurt m—"

Seamus felt his cyclone react urgently. In a split second, Seamus jabbed his heel on top of Davy's foot.

Davy yelped like a puppy.

"Stop that crying!" Mrs. Maidmill said, unaware of what was happening.

Seamus pressed harder for good measure and kept his foot on Davy's as he made one last attempt to tell his story.

"Seamus is hurting me!"

"Stop it right now, buster! Seamus is sitting like a good boy. I'm beginning to think he had nothing to do with disrupting my class. Seamus!"

"What, Mrs. Maidmill?"

"I think you should go out and play, don't you?" As soon as she said, "Good boy," Seamus's cyclone responded pleasantly.

There was no more pain. Seamus smiled at Mrs. Maidmill.

"Go on. You only have a few minutes before recess is over. Davy and I need to have a talk about rules." Her voice sharpened.

Seamus jabbed his heel one last time without her knowledge to send Davy into frenzy. Perhaps even if she was aware, she didn't care.

Davy sobbed louder as Seamus reached the door.

Seamus watched in silent victory as Mrs. Maidmill dragged him into the closet. The warm, spring sunshine pierced through the dirty glass on the door leading to the playground. Seamus was sure the light would soon consume him and take him to his next destination. Seamus inhaled a deep breath.

As his feet touched the poorly drawn hopscotch squares on the sidewalk, he opened his eyes and saw he was still in his six-year-old body. *Why am I still here?* Seamus felt a thick hand grab his shoulder.

Ms. Nungester, the recess attendant, stood over him. "What do you think you're doing, Bruiser?" she asked warmly. Ms. Nungester always referred to him as *Bruiser*. She was the only faculty member of Graham Elementary who was kind to him.

"Mrs. Maidmill kept me back for a while. Davy was bad, and she had to talk to both of us." Seamus spoke with a child's words.

Ms. Nungester's face soured from mentioning Mrs. Maidmill. They behaved cordial toward each other, but it was clear to everyone, including the children, they really did not get along. Ms. Nungester shifted her expression from sour to ornery. "So, mean old Mrs. Buster kept you back?" Ms. Nungester asked playfully.

Seamus returned the ornery smile. "You could say that again, Mrs. Buster Brown." Seamus laughed.

"*Buster Brown.* I can't believe I didn't think of that." Ms. Nungester laughed.

"Go and play, Bruiser. There isn't much time left, and from the sounds of it, you've earned it. You should get all the running around out of your system while you can or else Mrs. Maidmill might get *a might mad.*"

Seamus nodded and ran toward the swing sets. His laughter was only a ruse. During the exchange, all he could think was why was he still here? He feared he may be trapped. *I thought I fixed everything. What else could there be?* The question continued as his young heart thumped.

Sounds of taunting children from the trees on the edge of the playground broke his concentration. Seamus couldn't understand what they were saying, but he knew his classmates were tormenting another. Just as Seamus grew close, he heard Lynette sobbing. Seamus stood behind the ring of children as they continued.

"*Dummy, dummy, dumb,*" the children chanted as Lynette stood helpless.

"She looks like poop!" one boy shouted.

"She smells like it too," another said.

A well-dressed boy from his class entered the circle and looked down at her.

Seamus watched with disgust as he identified the boy through the fuzziness—Jake Chapnan, a pompous boy from a well-to-do family who lived in Bradford's prominent northside.

"Her family is poop too. They live in a poop house," Jake said.

"*Poop girl lives in poop house!*" the children chanted.

Seamus scanned the group, aghast.

Lynette looked like she would break into hysterics. Even though Jake's words were at a kindergarten level, they bore lasting cruelty.

Christ, I knew kids could be cruel, but this is just fucking crazy. I wonder how the hell I only kicked some of their asses and didn't kill them, especially that uppity sack of shit. Rage boiled over Seamus—not the rage of a child but the rage of a man.

Lynette knelt with her hands raised, pleading for Jake to stop.

Jake's eyes gleamed as he searched his small mind for a crushing insult. "She's retarded. That's why she sits at the same table as Seamus and Davy. *Retard! Retard!*" Jake chanted, and the others joined. The children were mindless sheep blindly following their shepherd. Jake danced around Lynette, mocking her.

The children were so deep in the throes of their chants, they didn't notice Seamus step forward. *This is the second time I've had to rescue her. Wait a minute, that happened in the future.* Seamus bulldozed his way through the ring of children.

The kids in the back fell silent. The stillness eventually spread to the front.

Jake's smile drooped when he became face to face with Seamus. In a last-ditch effort, Jake scrambled to reignite his companions. "Ooh, it looks like Lynette has a boyfriend!"

The children remained speechless as they sensed something new about Seamus—a presence Jake was too blind to see in his own hubris.

"Mrs. Maidmill put you together because you're retards. That's why you're not allowed to sit with anyone else."

"You better stop Jake or else."

"Or else what, ret—?"

Seamus grabbed Jake's shirt and shoved him to the ground.

Jake was covered in a cloud of dust. "I'm telling Mrs. Maidmill!"

Seamus picked up Jake again and flung him to the ground.

Jake's pride was crushed.

Seamus brought Jake to his feet as tears streaked his dusty face. "Go ahead and tell! If you do, I'll tell on all of you! Lynette will tell too!" Seamus surveyed his classmates and recognized some of them, while others were only stock faces who faded in his memories. Seamus chose his words carefully; he did not want to sound overly grown up.

They knew Seamus meant what he had said, and Lynette would confirm it. They walked away, breaking the circle.

Jake's lips quivered as he rubbed his eyes and acknowledged. He may not have understood what he was doing was wrong, but he acknowledged nonetheless. His own shattered pride was all he could comprehend. Even at a young age, Jake's pride was placed higher than the opinion of his flock. He would hold this mindset for the rest of his life, until it ended when he rolled his IROC during his junior year of high school. The only memory of Jake Chapnan was a memorial at the end zone of the high school football field. Shortly after his death, the players took a small running knee and touched it before each home game. The future athletes didn't even bother. His name and memory was eventually forgotten.

The children left as the recess whistle sounded, but Seamus and Lynette remained as she dried her eyes. Seamus asked if she was all right, and she blindsided him with a hug. As she sobbed again, Seamus returned the embrace.

"You'll be okay, Lynette. They won't pick on you anymore."

"Thank you, Seamus." Lynette backed away.

Seamus remembered what had happened between them in the future and all the other things that had happened to her during her life. A strange urge engulfed him as he gazed into her simple eyes. He needed to tell her something—a message from the future. Seamus wondered whether she would understand. Regardless, he still needed to say it. "No matter how bad people treat you, know you're worth being loved."

"Thank you Seamus." A toothy smile stretched across her face.

Ms. Nungester blew the whistle again.

Seamus nodded confidently and led the way to the building. He only paused briefly before proffering his hand.

Lynette's delicate hand joined his as they walked.

Once he and Lynette fell into line, a whitish-gold light greeted him. His cyclone swirled clockwise. Astonishment gripped him; this was the first time it had moved clockwise. *This had nothing to do with Davy. This was all about Lynette,* Seamus realized while he settled into the realm of light. Once the light had completely enveloped him, the image of the triangular orb that powered the prism met him from above.

It stopped once it reached eye level and cycled through its flashing colors—white, green, purple, and blue. A computerized and feminine voice followed shortly after. "You've made the necessary corrections. It's time for you to pass through and see what waits beyond."

Seamus acknowledged as the orb pulled him into the mysterious void. He closed his new eyes as he traveled through the heart of the orb. His old life was over. What lies beyond?

Chapter 11
A Call from the Past

Seamus's eyes remained closed as the light faded around him. He now inhabited a new body. When or wherever he was, he knew he was resting in a reclined position. Reluctantly, he opened his eyes as the sounds of his surroundings sprung into life. As the events unfolded, he gazed around, awestruck. Seamus was, in fact, sitting in a recliner in his house, but this was not his house on Observation Drive. This was the house from the vision he'd had in his bathroom mirror—the beautiful *mirage/dream* where he had seen his wife and children.

The world was motionless. The children were lying on their bellies, watching a frozen television screen. The beautiful wavy blond-haired woman from his dream sat to his left on the couch. Overwhelming joy filled Seamus.

The cyclone residing behind his chest dispersed through his limbs before the sensation rested behind his eyes. He was graced with visions of the past. It was not the past of his normal life but the events of his new life. It started with the day in kindergarten when he had prevented Davy Mueller from causing trouble. Images of him doing well in school as a child followed.

The memories progressed through his junior high school and high school years. While attending high school, he had participated in post-secondary education options, where he attended college at Rawling Springs State University. During this time, he had met Ricky Kerr, who was also attending the college. This was the first time in Seamus's life he'd had a true friend.

Seamus witnessed his high school graduation. He had graduated with honors and had been accepted into Rawling Springs State University on a full ride scholarship, where he majored in business management. Ricky had attended there as well, majoring in architecture. Together they had rented an off-campus apartment and enjoyed the college lifestyle. Seamus's memories carried him to another commencement ceremony where he had received his bachelor's degree. The visions continued into the next day following his graduation. He and Ricky had taken a trip to Fremont Bay and boarded the island ferry to Heinemann Island.

They had toured the island all day until they wound up at the Double Barrel Saloon for drinks. While he and Ricky were cutting loose, Seamus's attention was drawn to the striking vision of his future wife wearing a white sundress and coated with a tan.

After their eyes met from across the dance floor, she approached him with unwavering determination. She traversed across the bar and introduced herself—Melody Greene.

Seamus returned the introduction before the two stepped onto the patio.

Ricky joined them until he could see things were going well for Seamus. Ricky wished his friend good luck and patted his shoulder before returning inside.

Melody and Seamus strolled around the island. Seamus told her he had recently graduated from Rawling Springs State University with a bachelor's degree.

Melody told him she had just received her bachelor's degree in office administration from Port Lucas University. They continued to talk about life as they walked the narrow streets. She told Seamus she was from Perryslanding.

Seamus was familiar with the wealthy town located north of Rawling Springs.

She also told Seamus she was rooming with some friends from college.

Seamus withheld the information about Bradford; he only told her he lived in Rawling Springs.

Melody told him she had a job in place as an office associate at Cardinal Solar Panel Manufacturing.

Seamus took the opportunity to play a joke. He told her he had no clue what he was going to do. In truth, he already had a fully-fledged plan. Ricky's parents had provided him and Ricky a large amount of money to start their own construction business. The business would be K&V Construction. Seamus watched as Melody's face became forlorn. Seamus could not hold the guise for long and erupted with laughter.

Melody was pleased that he had a plan.

They continued their walk and conversation as the moonlight gleamed over them. Seamus made a lasting comment as he saw Melody in a new light. "You've never looked better in my eyes."

It was the sweetest and most random thing she'd ever heard. Melody stopped in her tracks and looked to her right.

Seamus beheld her with stars in his eyes.

Melody's attention was drawn to a single-story, ivory-colored structure.

Seamus eyed it curiously and wondered why she was taken by the building. To him, it resembled a basic, run-of-the-mill chapel o' love.

Melody commented on how romantic it would be to have her wedding there. After looking at the small chapel together, they returned to the bar.

Seamus reconnected with Ricky, and Melody did likewise with her friends. Seamus did not remember seeing her with friends earlier. He must have been intently caught up in her beauty. Seamus and Melody rode the last ferry to Fremont Bay. After they docked, they exchanged a passionate kiss, along with their phone numbers.

Naturally, her friends teased her on the ride home, and Ricky did likewise to Seamus. While each traveled home, they only thought of their time together on the island.

The memory of the island excursion was not the end of Seamus's visions. He was blessed with the events that came after. Melody and Seamus's romance grew, along with his and Ricky's business. Seamus also watched as their wedding day came to be. Just as Melody had wanted, they were married in the small chapel on Heinemann Island. Seamus said the same words to her as he had during their first night together. "You've never looked better in my eyes."

Although the venue was small and stuffy, it was a beautiful ceremony. Ricky stood alongside Seamus as his best man, and Melody's friends from the night they had first met were her bridesmaids. Seamus and Melody both noticed the sparks that flew between Ricky and Melody's friend, Sarah.

The memories of meeting Melody and marrying her were the beginning of Seamus's bliss. Shortly after Seamus and Melody were wed, the construction of their new home in the rural country south of Perryslanding began. Once construction was complete, Melody told Seamus she was pregnant while they enjoyed an intimate supper together. Memories of Melody's pregnancy and the birth of their twins, Brianna and Brian, flooded his mind. Brianna was born first, and Brian followed three minutes after. Seamus watched as his children grew and developed into their current age.

The visions ended just as Seamus was brought up to speed on his current life. His final memory was of his mother, something she had said to him before she and his father had died in their accident in his old life. *"Right before a person dies, they see their life flash before their eyes."*

Seamus wondered if this was true when his parents had died and for Elizabeth and her lovers. Did their lives pass before their eyes? A haunting feeling came, but he dispelled it. Seamus had altered the events of his past; his parents were alive and, to the best of his knowledge, so were Elizabeth and her lovers. At least, they should be because he did not meet and kill them. Even if they weren't alive and someone else had … *Fuck it!* It wasn't his problem.

Seamus was jostled from his feelings of satisfaction as the world awoke. He shuffled nervously in his recliner as his surroundings gained motion. It started from the children's show on the television, expanded from the wall behind the set, before circumnavigating toward him and Melody.

Once life and movement resumed, Melody looked perplexed when she regarded Seamus.

Seamus was the only one aware the world was frozen. The children didn't miss a beat as they giggled over the old man and his house filled with balloons.

"Babe, are you feeling all right?" Melody whispered.

He couldn't tell her the truth. *I'm fine babe. I just traveled from an alternate timeline after I killed a couple of people, and then I was given a second chance at life. Plus, I had to wait for this reality to reboot, but other than that, I'm peachy.* Instead, he employed humor. "It might've been that dish you made. That health food shit disagrees with me."

"Don't say cuss words, Daddy!" Brianna shouted.

"Yeah, Dad!" Brian added.

"Daddy is just being a big old ass." Melody stuck out her tongue.

"Don't cuss, Mommy!" the twins said in unison.

"Watch your show. It's almost bedtime," Melody scolded playfully, then eyed her husband. "Are you sure everything's all right?"

"Everything's great. It couldn't be better. I was just thinking about something work related. Ricky and I have a project coming up." As the words left his mouth, Seamus hoped an upcoming project really existed. His grasp for straws paid off.

Melody gave a look of approval. "Maybe I should go back to work. The kids are getting older, and a little extra money wouldn't hurt."

"Absolutely not. I like having you home. I promised you I would support us. I love you. It's my job to take care of this family."

"I love you, Seamus."

"I always love you, Melody."

Melody told the children it was bedtime.

They only gave minimal protest before heading to the bathroom to brush their teeth.

Melody and Seamus tucked them in afterward, and Melody led Seamus down the hallway into their bedroom. Passion ignited as they pressed their lips.

Melody stepped backward and removed her clothes. It was a wonderful sight.

I can't believe all of this is mine. She is mine.

Melody ushered him to the bed.

He ogled at her ample body as he caressed her. They made love before each released a bountiful climax.

Melody peacefully collapsed in his arms.

Seamus cherished the warmth of her skin. They shared one last kiss before turning off the lights.

Life was good for Seamus. As time passed, Seamus and his family prospered. The twins grew into teenagers, and Melody looked the part of a woman ten years younger than she actually was. Just as Seamus's new life flashed before his eyes, the better side of a decade did as well. Seamus and Melody were now in their early forties, the twins were freshmen in high school, and K&V Construction was the leading construction company in the county.

Seamus reflected on his accomplishments as he drove home from work. He had never known true happiness in his old life. He had only regarded it as a foundation of something to avoid. His family could never know the truth of his origin.

However, foreboding memories soured his mood. Seamus remembered his original life's failures, court appearances, the acts he had committed with Lynette, but the murders disturbed him the most. *Why are they haunting me now? What does this mean? What do I have to do to escape that life forever?* His resolve strengthened as he made his final approach. *I will not allow this to happen. I'll be damned if I go back without a fight.* As the tires of his truck rolled onto his driveway, he had purged the thoughts—that was, until he parked.

Everything seemed normal when he stepped inside his house. The twins were in the family room. Brian was highlighting a textbook, and Brianna was talking to her boyfriend on the phone. Seamus and Melody thought things were getting too serious between Briana and her boyfriend, but they dismissed it as teenage love. Nothing seemed to be out of the ordinary, until he entered the kitchen. Seamus discovered Melody staring out the back kitchen window. It looked as if she had seen a ghost.

"How's my number one girl?" Seamus asked as Melody tightly wrapped her arms around him. "Jeez, Melody, you've never hugged me like that before. What's going on?"

Melody looked at her husband as if it was the first or last time.

Seamus released himself from her grasp. He led her to the oak kitchen table. Melody and Seamus sat across from each other as he eagerly waited to be filled in.

"After you went to work, I did a couple things around the house—the laundry, picked up a few items, and even did some much-needed dusting. I just went on a cleaning frenzy. I don't know what came over me."

"The place looks great, honey."

"I went to the grocery store afterward so we wouldn't have to do it together. I know you're not the biggest fan of shopping, so I decided to take care of it myself."

Seamus sat on the edge of his seat. "Did something happen at the store?"

"No, I didn't have any trouble. It was ... after that."

"What happened?" Seamus asked as his nerves crawled.

"I didn't see him—not until I made the first trip with the groceries."

"Who did you see?"

"A man was sitting on our front porch—a strange man. He looked like he was dressed in old-time clothes from the twenties or thirties. You know I'm not good with history."

Seamus's heart rose to his throat. "What did he want?"

"He said his name was Roland Hiser and that he was an independent businessman—an entrepreneur. Honey, it wasn't just the way he looked or the words he said, it was his voice—his accent; it was creepy. I was freaked the fuck out. You know me, I hardly ever cuss, but that's how I felt. The man genuinely freaked me the fuck out. I wanted to run back to the Buick and call the police."

"Did you call the police?"

"No, Seamus. That was the weird part. I froze to the ground. My feet would simply not move. When I final did move, it felt like I was being pulled. It was embarrassing, but I dropped the groceries where I stood. I don't know why I did. I couldn't help myself."

"What did he do?" Seamus shouted.

Melody gestured to lower his voice. "Nothing. He only talked to me, but it was the things he said ... scary things. I already told you he introduced himself as Roland Hiser and that he said he was an independent businessman. Roland said he had business with you. What he said next *really* terrified me. He said everything you are and have is because of him. He said you have a past life and did horrible things before he brought you out, that you were a murderer." Melody broke into tears.

"I've never killed anyone."

"There's no way you could have. I'm not saying that because I love you but because he said you did it around ten years ago in an—"

"An, what?"

"An alternate timeline or something. He said this life was only a ruse—a falsehood. You really don't belong here. I'm so scared." Melody sprung from her chair and wrapped her arms around Seamus.

Seamus reassured her that everything would be fine, that he would stay home with her and work from his office. Seamus promised Roland Hiser would not be a problem.

Melody went to the kitchen sink and splashed water on her face.

Roland had returned to collect the favor. *I won't let that bastard hurt you or the kids. I'll kill him if I have to.* Seamus stared out the kitchen window. Although fear weighed on him, he mustered a smile and hugged his wife.

Melody collapsed into his arms.

The wheels in Seamus's head turned.

After dinner, Seamus helped with the dishes, Brian and Brianna left to spend time with their friends, and Melody watched him with deep love. Seamus only looked out the window. Once the dishes were done, Seamus walked to his personal office to call Ricky. Seamus only included the details Ricky needed to hear.

"Hello, Seamus. What's going on?"

"Hey, Rickster. I wanted to let you know Melody is having some problems and needs me. I'll be working from home for a while. If things continue, I'll let you know, but, for now, I need to be home for her and the kids."

"Is something wrong? If there is, Sarah will twist my arm until I tell her."

"No, Ricky. Everything is fine. Melody just had a disturbing event and needs me. As soon as we get this straightened out, I'll be back in the office. If you need me, just call me at home."

"Likewise, buddy. If you need anything, don't hesitate. Sarah and I are here for you. If it wasn't for you and Melody, I never would've met Sarah. Besides, you remember what I always say; it's more than just meeting my wife—I always felt there was something else, but I never could put my finger on it."

Seamus knew exactly what it was. It was the time he had saved him from a severe beating from Chris Rayle and his mongoloid goons. Unfortunately for Ricky—or maybe fortunately after all—Ricky would never know. "Thanks, Ricky. You really are my best friend—my brother."

"Anytime, Seamus. Sarah and I are always here for your family. I've got to go, man. Sarah wants me to watch some goofy musical. Maybe if I can struggle through that, she'll be frisky. Have a good evening."

"Thanks, Ricky." Seamus hung up and sat in silence for the rest of the evening.

The week passed uneventful as Seamus worked from home. The children went to school, and Melody completed her daily tasks.

There were no more disturbances from Roland. Seamus felt calm by the end of the week. That was, until Friday after dinner.

Seamus and his family gathered at the table and indulged in a delicious meatloaf. Brianna and Brian were receiving high marks in school, and Brianna and her boyfriend were easing up. Brian had been invited to play keyboard and bass guitar in a garage band with some of his school chums, and Melody seemed restored to her typical self.

The twins excused themselves from the table and dispersed to their rooms.

Melody and Seamus washed the dishes and enjoyed pleasant conversation. Seamus excused himself and told her he still had some work to finish.

Melody playfully whipped him with her towel.

Just as Seamus sat behind his desk, his ease was broken when his phone rang. Seamus checked the caller ID and felt ill. He couldn't identify the number but could tell by the area code and the prefix that it was a Bradford number. The words Hollow Grove inhabited his mind.

"Hello, my good man. How've you been?" a man asked casually.

"Who is this?"

"It's none other than Roland Hiser. I know it's been a long time, but I was sure you wouldn't forget me. I came by to visit you the other day, but you must have been out. However, I did meet your missus. Unfortunately, I didn't have the privilege of meeting the children."

"Stay away from me and my family!"

"Come now, Seamus, I don't mean you or them harm. I just remembered the bargain we made. I gave you what you wanted, and, from the looks of your home and your wife, you've done well. I said the day would come when I would ask for a favor. Not that I'm a man of threats, but, if you wish to keep your happy home intact, I suggest we have a nice little reunion." Roland's voice sounded demonic.

"Where do you want to meet, you sonofabitch?" Seamus hissed.

"There's no need for profanity. After all, I'm the one who has given you so much. You could say we're best friends—like brothers." Roland's voice returned to normal.

Seamus felt ill as Roland said *best friends* and *brother*.

"There's only one place I can think befitting for our long, overdo reunion. I think if you search your mind, the answer will hit you like a ton of bricks—maybe not bricks but cobblestone." Roland bellowed with a demonic laugh.

"Hollow Grove."

"Right-o, my good man."

"When do you want to meet, you cocksucker?"

"Why don't we meet tonight at midnight? It'll be a new day and a new beginning for our renewed partnership. I'm looking forward to seeing you."

Seamus slammed the receiver. After pounding his desk, he checked the clock—6:45 p.m. Seamus would not face him unprepared. In a quick decision, he called Ricky. "Hello, Ricky. I need your help."

"What's going on?"

"Can I stop by?"

"What do you need?"

"I need a gun."

"What the hell do you need with a gun?"

"I need to protect my family. Melody won't let me keep one in the house, and I know you have a few."

"What if it falls into the wrong hands? Can't you just call the police?"

"What if the police can't make it in time? I need something to protect them."

"Okay, Seamus. I'll loan you a gun, but if it gets used for something other than home protection, I will report it stolen. Do you understand?"

"I understand."

"When do you need it?"

"I'll be on my way as soon as we hang up."

"Okay, I'll see you soon."

Seamus collected some old documents to use as an excuse to leave and headed toward the living room. "Hey, honey, I ran into some work issues, and I need to see Ricky."

"Can't you straighten it out over the phone?"

"No. This needs to be taken care of in person. I won't be long." He leaned over and kissed his wife.

"Okay, I love you."

"I always love you, Melody."

Seamus left in a dead sprint. He drove through Perryslanding and reached the other side of town by 7:20 p.m. As he pulled into Ricky's driveway, he noticed Ricky's house was more immaculate than his. Seamus wondered if it had anything to do with his success or if Ricky would have done fine without him. Now was not the time to contemplate that.

Ricky was standing outside.

Seamus stepped from his truck with the old documents in his hand.

"Here it is, Seamus. It's an SAR ST 10." Ricky briefed Seamus about the gun, including the components, the location of the safety, and the magazine release.

Seamus assured Ricky he remembered everything he had taught him during their time at the shooting range.

Ricky handed the gun to Seamus, and Seamus handed him the documents. "Why are you giving me these old reports?"

"I needed an excuse to get out of the house, so I used them as a prop."

"I hope I haven't made a mistake," Ricky said somberly.

"You didn't. I just need to protect my family."

"Just remember what I said."

"I will. Thank you again," Seamus said before he walked away. He concealed the weapon inside the toolbox compartment in the truck bed.

He returned home at 7:45 p.m. and enjoyed a quiet evening with his family. The hours flew like seconds. Shortly after 10:00 p.m., his children called it a night. Just as they were about to head to bed, Seamus told them to stop.

The children eyed each other curiously.

Seamus took one last look at them and said he loved them.

They told him the same before they climbed the steps.

Melody asked if he was feeling all right.

He assured her he was fine; he was only feeling sentimental.

Melody was moved by Seamus's declaration.

Around 10:40 p.m., they went upstairs, where they made love until Melody fell asleep. At 11:25 p.m., once he was sure she was fully asleep, Seamus slid from bed and got dressed. He turned back one last time to behold his wife. He would do anything to see her like this always.

Seamus descended the stairs, stepped through the front door, and locked it behind him. It was 11:30p.m. He had thirty minutes to get to Hollow Grove. This would hopefully be the last time in either his old life or his new life when he would see the place. Whether this trip would go in his favor or not, he did not know. All he knew was his business with Roland would be done, forever.

CHAPTER 12
LEAVING HOLLOW GROVE

Seamus's eyes were glued to the road, but his thoughts were surrounded by his past. *Why is this happening? What does Roland want?* The thoughts intensified as Perryslanding faded in his mirrors. This would be the last time he saw the community. Seamus wished for nothing more than to return home. The urge to pull over and observe a moment of silence compelled him. Roland had only given him a taste of the good life.

Seamus's hate for Roland grew as he traveled. Thoughts of killing Roland gave him pleasure. It was Roland who should have died, not the others. No one in his entire life, past or present, had made him suffer as much as Roland had. Seamus wondered if meeting Elizabeth had all been part of Roland's design. Why stop there? Maybe everything had Roland's name on it. It all made perfect sense.

If he had the power to give him a new life, he had the power to fuck up his original life. *Roland used me! I'm a goddamn puppet. Once he's done, I lose everything.*

Hollow Grove came into view in a nest of shadows. Fear nearly crippled Seamus. He tried to rationalize that his fear lies with Roland's schemes alone, but that was only half true. The building itself was evil. It had to be to accommodate a monster like Roland. Seamus slowed his truck to a crawl.

He wanted to take Roland by surprise—not just Roland but Hollow Grove. It was a foolish thought. If Roland and Hollow Grove were truly marred with evil, then they already knew he was there. Seamus glanced at the time—11:57 p.m.

Seamus paused to do something he'd never thought before; he wanted to take one last look at himself. After inspecting his reflection, he stepped into the night. Before he headed to the building, he retrieved the handgun and studied the magazine. Seamus didn't know whether bullets would work on Roland.

A brisk wind struck Seamus's face as he approached the fence. As much as he tried to rebuke the thought, he could not help to feel something supernatural. As the wind blew, eerie voices echoed from his original life. Seamus concentrated on the voices of his parents, conversations between him and Elizabeth, Lynette's declarations of love, and Roland's voice requesting a favor.

Roland's voice faded as the sound of the wind returned. A humorless grin stretched over Seamus' face. *If he's trying to freak me out, he is sorely mistaken.* Seamus maintained bravery as the aged entrance door stood to his left.

Seamus never regarded the door as anything more than just an entrance to the watering hole, but this time, it looked like a gateway to Hell. As he opened the door, it did the rest for him. Seamus carefully entered the void. He half expected the door to slam shut. Instead, the door only swayed with the intermittent breeze.

The moonlight from outside guided his way. The place looked as it had when Mack had owned it. Nothing indicated Roland's remodeling. Seamus walked toward the middle.

Light shone from behind the door marked **Private**. While walking on the cracked floor, he watched the light pulse white, green, purple, and blue.

Roland awaited upstairs.

The radiant light ceased, and the door creaked open. The staircase was pitch black. *You couldn't leave the light on for me? Fucking prick.* The dilapidated steps creaked under his feet. Seamus paused halfway and concealed the handgun in his waist. If Roland could be full of surprises, then maybe he could too. Seamus envisioned Roland's face as a bullet slammed into his forehead.

As he neared the top of the staircase, the haunting pattern of light greeted him. The glowing light became something that defined him.

Seamus had little time for mental collection. He was face to face with the machine that was his blessing and curse. It was exactly as he remembered it—quite in fact, the entire room appeared the same. It was only the downstairs that had been affected by unforgiving time.

Just as Seamus was about to call out, he was halted.

Roland stepped from behind the prism.

Contempt overwhelmed Seamus. All he wanted was to kill first and ask questions later.

Seamus's hatred intoxicated Roland with baleful pleasure. Roland extended his arms toward him and broke Seamus's bitter gaze. "Seamus, it's been far too long."

"Get your goddamn hands off me!" Roland backpedaled with a frown.

Roland's expression exploded into a maniacal smile. He was not done tormenting Seamus. "Is that any way to treat an old friend? This could have all been sorted out. I made an effort to discuss the matter with you the day I met your wife. She is an exquisite vision, but I'm sure you already know that."

Seamus couldn't hold back and punched Roland's jaw.

The force nearly knocked down Roland, but his body snapped back with unnatural reflex. A look of shock rested on his face. He countered with a choke hold and raised Seamus off the ground. Roland's true face flickered like a hologram.

Seamus gasped.

Once control was returned to his favor, he lowered Seamus. "I'm not something to be trifled with," Roland snarled.

"Something? Don't you mean *someone*?" Seamus asked, clasping his throat.

"*Someone* would mean I'm human. That condition no longer applies; I haven't been bound to those limitations for a long time."

"What are you?"

"I'm the next leap in evolution. Do you understand what I'm saying? If you couldn't assume I'm from a different time by the manner of my speech and my attire, then you're fundamentally stupid." Roland waited for Seamus to follow with the obvious question.

"Where the hell are you from?"

"That's the correct question. I also appreciate that you emphasized Hell. That loathsome place plays an important role. Before I became what I am now, I was human. I lived and thrived in the nineteen thirties. Most people during that time were experiencing the hardship of the Great Depression. Much to my chagrin, my prosperity was shared with a partner—my original partner."

"Get to the fucking point, Rollie. What does this have to do with me?"

"Patience, you insipid little shit! I'm getting to that! If you ever call me Rollie again, I'll make Hell seem like a pleasure cruise!"

"Spill it, you bastard!"

"Toward the end of my natural life, I lived in the thirties. Actually, I resided in Rawling Springs where my partner and I ran a successful bijou theater. Oh yes, the Cla-Zel was an illustrious place. Things were going well for Harlan and me—that was until thirty-nine. Some might still refer to it as Hollywood's greatest year of film. It was August twenty-fifth, to be exact. We had a triumphant success with the premier of *The Wizard of Oz*. That was when Harlan introduced me to his new lover—his muse, Christine. I was smitten by her beauty as she stood before me in her silken, ruby dress. However, I was more smitten by her necklace."

"What does a woman's necklace have to do with anything?"

"That's the funny part. Christine was wearing both the orbs like jewelry. The orb of time and science, along with magic and fantasy, were dangling in front of me. A voice came to me in a dream that night. It encouraged me to take Christine and the orbs. The following evening was when I discovered the identity of the voice—Mr. Murphy. He told me the truth and the power the orbs held—a power that had to be mine. I phoned Harlan the following morning and told him I had much to discuss after the theater closed the next evening. I told him I had new ideas. I just neglected to tell him my ideas didn't include him. After the theater closed, we met in the office. Unfortunately, Christine was there by his side. It was supposed to be clean and simple; it was supposed to be between us partners!"

"What did you do?"

Roland withdrew a strange pistol from his coat. "I killed my partner. I shot him with my trusty Mauser C96. Once he fell, Christine knelt desperately beside him. That was when the situation became peculiar."

"What happened?"

"The bitch dangled her necklace over Harlan's body. I wanted to take her for myself, but the voice in my dream ordered me to kill her and make off with the orbs. As I approached, she looked at me, and her eyes lit up. I was thrown out of the office, and the door slammed shut. I tried to force it open. After the third try, I saw smoke billowing from the cracks. When I forced it open, the room was engulfed, and Christine evaporated into thin air. The only thing that remained of her was the orb of time and science. I watched as it fell to Harlan's chest. The orb of magic and fantasy was nowhere in sight. I raced over to collect the remaining orb. By the time I had it in my hand, the office became too difficult to cross. I was petrified when I saw the images projecting from across the room in Harlan's Tudor mirror. I saw my descent into Hell. Before I succumbed to hellfire, Mr. Murphy stepped from the mirror."

"What does this have to do with the favor?"

"I gave you a new life, so you owe me a new life."

"What do you want?"

"You must kill the descendant of Harlan Burks. His great nephew, James Burks, possesses what is rightfully mine. You can find him in Swanta. How convenient is that? If my geography is correct, all you must do is go to the next town over from where you live.

"I can't kill anybody!"

"If you don't, I'll kill your family, or do something worse; I'll rescind our deal. You'll return to your old life and stand trial for murder. Maybe it won't be so bad; you only killed one person, after all." Roland grinned.

"One person? I killed three people before I came to you."

"Elizabeth and Chelsea escaped and watched you drive away. They could identify you as Josh's murderer." Roland erupted into laughter. "There's no way to evade murder. The act follows a man from one life to another. I'm sorry I forgot to mention that to you. Murder has a profound effect. If you commit it in one life, you must commit it in another. Even though you would not be killing the same person, you must kill to keep the balance. It all boils down to same act/different venue. As someone who used to be in the theater business, I can tell you all about venues. Kill him with this." Roland tossed the Mauser C96 to Seamus.

"Why would I have to kill him with this?"

"It's the condition Mr. Murphy laid upon me when he pulled me from Hell. Trust me, it'll benefit us both."

"How does is this benefit both of us? Why can't you kill him?"

"As I said before, it's the condition Mr. Murphy set in place. Even if I wanted to kill James, I can't. I'm bound to Mr. Murphy's rules. It's physically impossible for me to pull the trigger. As far as it benefitting both of us, that's simple. You'll be released from me, and I'll be released from Mr. Murphy. I'll possess both orbs, and the third will soon be in my possession. You have no choice. It's your destiny. That's the reason I found you. I found you on the day you were born. I could sense you were destined to be a killer. Kill for me! Kill for your family! Kill for your own good. Kill James Burks and set us free. You have everything to gain. Do it!"

Seamus felt hatred for the weapon. *If I must kill, why don't I just kill Roland? You know better, Seamus. If you use his weapon on him, the bullet will just go right through him.*

Roland eagerly awaited Seamus's decision.

Seamus knew what had to be done. He threw the Mauser C96 at Roland.

It struck him on his forearm as he made a defensive move.

Seamus readied his gun while Roland was distracted. He pointed it at the top of the prism and fired. The machine component burst into a frenzy of sparks. The prism walls vanished.

Roland released an earth-shattering scream as his body lost density. His outline flashed in the same color pattern as the orb. "You've ruined everything!"

Seamus dropped his gun and fell to his knees. The triangular orb hovered in front of Seamus.

"Thank you for releasing me," the ethereal voice said. "My power doesn't belong to Roland; it never did. My power doesn't belong to you either. I'm grateful for what you've done, but I can't return you. The life you've been living does not belong to you. I can't allow you to remain."

"I know," Seamus said glumly.

"You must return something."

Seamus nodded a single time and studied the center of the object.

Before the reversal process started, the orb spoke again. "Maybe I can give you something else in return. Take heed; you only have one chance."

Without breaking eye contact with the orb, Seamus felt his cyclone spin counterclockwise. His new body dissolved, along with Roland's laboratory. He closed his eyes and traveled to the other side.

Seamus found himself sitting at Hollow Grove. It was not the dilapidated version of the place, nor was it Roland's Shooting Shark. This was the Hollow Grove from his original time.

Mack stood in front of him. "What are you sitting there like a bump in a log for, Seamus?"

"What?"

"I'm cutting you off."

Seamus was never happier to see Mack. "I think you're right. I've had enough."

"Take a walk."

Seamus did not reply. He turned from the bar. His attention was drawn to the row of chairs facing the pool table.

Sweeney's friends were discussing that Sweeney had bit off more than he could chew with what he planned on doing with that woman.

Seamus realized he was reliving the night he had met Elizabeth. He dashed quickly toward the entrance. Just as Seamus predicted, Elizabeth was standing by the lamppost, talking on her phone, while Sweeney harassed her. Normally, Seamus would have intervened, but his reserve kept him glued to the spot.

Sweeney flung Elizabeth's phone to the ground, and Elizabeth screamed while Sweeney forced her against his truck. Elizabeth locked eyes with Seamus.

Seamus only offered her a modest wave.

Sweeney opened his truck's passenger door and forced her inside.

Elizabeth fought desperately for freedom. Her screams grew muffled as Sweeney's truck rocked.

Seamus approached the fence and stopped just as he passed the missing boards. A strange buzzing came from his pocket. He withdrew a pointy object—the orb of time and science. Its transitioning colors intensified into a solid whitish gold.

"You've done well to heed my warning. Now give me something in return. Search your heart; you know what to do."

Warm tears fell from Seamus's eyes on the cool, misty night. Carefully, he scanned the lot and eyed Sweeney's truck.

It was still rocking while Elizabeth screamed, "Stop raping me! I didn't ask for this!"

Seamus surveyed the orb and closed his fist. He peeked through the gap in the fence and threw the orb. He thought he heard an expression of gratitude. Before leaving, he turned to look at Hollow Grove for the last time.

TER 1

.